M000073679

Contents

Ruskin Bond has been writing for over sixty years, and has now over 120 titles in print—novels, collections of stories, poetry, essays, anthologies and books for children. His first novel, *The Room on the Roof*, received the prestigious John Llewellyn Rhys award in 1957. He has also received the Padma Shri (1999), the Padma Bhushan (2014) and two awards from the Sahitya Akademi—one for his short stories and another for his writings for children. In 2012, the Delhi government gave him its Lifetime Achievement award.

Born in 1934, Ruskin Bond grew up in Jamnagar, Shimla, New Delhi and Dehradun. Apart from three years in the UK, he has spent all his life in India, and now lives in Mussoorie with his adopted family.

A shy person, Ruskin says he likes being a writer because 'When I'm writing there's nobody watching me. Today, it's hard to find a profession where you're not being watched!'

By the same author:

All Roads
Lead to Ganga

Ruskin Bond

RUPA

Published by
Rupa Publications India Pvt. Ltd 1992, 2007
7/16, Ansari Road, Daryaganj
New Delhi 110002

Sales centres:
Allahabad Bengaluru Chennai
Hyderabad Jaipur Kathmandu
Kolkata Mumbai

ISBN: 978-81-291-1213-2

Seventh impression 2014

10 9 8 7

The moral right of the author has been asserted.

Typeset by Mindways Design, New Delhi

Printed at Yash Printographics, Noida

The Writer on the Hill

IT'S HARD TO REALISE THAT I'VE BEEN HERE ALL THESE years—forty summers and monsoons and winters and Himalayan springs—because, when I look back to the time of my first coming here, it really does seem like yesterday.

That probably sums it all up. Time passes, and yet it doesn't pass (it is only you and I who are passing). People come and go, the mountains remain. Mountains are permanent things. They are stubborn, they refuse to move. You can blast holes out of them for their mineral wealth; or strip them of their trees and foliage; or dam their streams and divert their torrents; or make tunnels and roads and bridges; but no matter how hard they try, humans cannot actually get rid of these mountains. That's what I like about them; they are here to stay.

I like to think that I have become a part of this mountain, this particular range, and that by living here for so long, I am able to claim a relationship with the trees, wild flowers, even the rocks that are an integral part of it. Yesterday, at twilight, when I passed beneath the canopy of oak leaves, I felt that I was a part of the forest. I put out my hand and touched the bark of an old tree and as I turned away, its leaves brushed against my face as if to acknowledge me.

One day I thought, if we trouble these great creatures too much, and hack away at them and destroy their young, they will simply uproot themselves and march away— whole forests on the move—over the next range and the next, far from the haunts of man. Over the years, I have seen many forests and green places dwindle and disappear.

Now there is an outcry. It is suddenly fashionable to be an environmentalist. That's all right. Perhaps it isn't too late to save the little that's left. They could start by curbing the property developers, who have been spreading their tentacles far and wide.

The sea has been celebrated by many great writers— Conrad, Melville, Stevenson, Masefield—but I cannot think of anyone comparable for whom the mountains have been a recurring theme. I must turn to the Taoist poets from old China to find a true feeling for mountains. Kipling does occasionally look to the hills, but the Himalayas do not appear to have given rise to any memorable Indian literature, at least not in modern times.

By and large, I suppose, writers have to stay in the plains to make a living. Hill people have their work cut out just trying to wrest a livelihood from their thin, calcinated soil.

And as for mountaineers, they climb their peaks and move on, in search of other peaks; they do not take up residence in the mountains.

But to me, as a writer, the mountains have been kind. They were kind from the beginning, when I threw up a job in Delhi and rented a small cottage on the outskirts of the hill-station. Today, most hill-stations are rich men's playgrounds, but twenty-five years ago, they were places where people of modest means could live quite cheaply. There were very few cars and everyone walked about.

The cottage was situated on the edge of an oak and maple forest and I spent eight or nine years in it, most of them happy years, writing stories, essays, poems, books for children. It was only after I came to live in the hills that I began writing for children.

I think this had something to do with Prem's children. Prem Singh came to work for me as a boy, fresh from his village near Rudraprayag, in Pauri Garhwal. He was taller and darker than most of the young men from his area. Although in those days the village school did not go beyond the primary stage, he had an aptitude for reading and a good head for figures.

After he had been with me for a couple of years, he went home to get married, and then he and his wife Chandra took on the job of looking after the house and all practical matters; I remain helpless with electric-fuses, clogged cisterns, leaking gas cylinders, ruptured water-pipes, tin roofs that blow away whenever there's a storm, and the do-it-yourself world of hill-station India. In other words, they made it possible for a writer to write.

They also nursed me when I was ill, and gave me a feeling of belonging to a family, something which I hadn't known since childhood.

Their sons Rakesh and Mukesh, and daughter Savitri, grew up in Maplewood Cottage and then in other houses and cottages when we moved. I became, for them, an adopted grandfather. For Rakesh I wrote a story about a cherry tree that had difficulty in growing up (he was rather frail as a child). For Mukesh, who liked upheavals, I wrote a story about an earthquake and put him in it; and for Savitri I wrote a whole bunch of rhymes and poems.

One seldom ran short of material. There was a stream at the bottom of the hill and this gave me many subjects in the way of small (occasionally large) animals, wild flowers, birds, trees, insects, ferns. The nearby villages were of absorbing interest. So were the old houses and old families of the Landour and Mussoorie hill-stations.

There were walks into the mountains and along the pilgrim trails, and sometimes I slept at a roadside tea-shop or at a village school. Sadly, many of these villages are still without basic medical and educational facilities taken for granted elsewhere.

'Who goes to the hills, goes to his mother.' So wrote Kipling in Kim and he seldom wrote truer words, for living in the hills was like living in the bosom of a strong, sometimes proud, but always comforting, mother. And every time I went away, the homecoming would be more tender and precious. It became increasingly difficult for me to go away. Once the mountains are in your blood, there is no escape.

It has not always been happiness and light. Two-year old Suresh (who came between Rakesh and Mukesh) died of tetanus. I had bouts of ill-health, and there were times when money ran out. Freelancing can be daunting at times, and I never could make enough to buy a house like almost everyone else I know.

Editorial doors close; but when one door closes, another has, for me, almost immediately, miraculously opened. I could perhaps have done a little better living in London or Hong Kong, or even Bombay. But given the choice, I would not have done differently. When you have received love from people and the freedom that only the mountains can give, you have come very near the borders of heaven.

And now, Rakesh and Beena have three lovely children, and Mukesh and Vinita have two little scamps.

Rani of the Doon

REMEMBERING THE DEHRA DUN OF MY BOYHOOD IN the 1940s, with its modest population of about forty thousand souls, and contemplating it now, with a population of roughly five lakh persons, I cannot help tossing a question into the void and asking the Creator, 'God, what will it be twenty years from now?'

To this God, as enigmatic as ever, replies: 'A computer should be able to tell you. Find out for yourself.'

All the same, for one who presumably created our earth and all that moves upon it, it must be a little daunting to observe the growth of mankind (in sheer numbers), often at the expense of other creatures and the forest and plant life that has sustained us. God may be forgiving, but Nature is not, and we upset the ecological balance at our own peril.

To take this one small corner of the world, this particular valley, it is fascinating to realise that just four hundred years ago the only habitations were a few scattered villages.

It is possible to identify them, although they have long since been swallowed up in urban Dehra Dun. In the late sixteenth and early seventeenth centuries, the Doon was governed by a woman, Rani Karnavati, who apparently administered the territory on behalf of the Garhwal rajas. Her consort, a certain Abju Kanwar, was content to remain in the background. Early records mention that her palace was at a place called Nawada, on Nagsidh hill, a few miles south-east of the present city.

Included in her domain were the villages of Kaulagarh, Karnapur, Rajpur and Kyarkuli. Karnapur and Kaulagarh have long since been absorbed into the city. Guru Ram Rai's settlement at Khurbura in the late seventeenth century started the process. Rajpur remained a separate hamlet until it became a staging post on the way to Mussoorie, when that hill-station was founded by the British in the 1820s.

Only Kyarkuli has remained more or less aloof from both Dehra and Mussoorie. You can see it straddling its own ridge as you drive up to Mussoorie; almost, but not quite, swallowed up by the limestone quarries that had until recently spread like a cancer over the hills.

Rani Karnavati must have been an outstanding woman in her time. She is credited with having built the original Rajpur canal, which was later restored by the British to water their tea-estates and lichi gardens. Atkinson, in his *Gazetteer*, tells us that on a peak in the Dudatoli range there is a temple of Shiva at Binsar; a temple celebrated throughout the lower foot-hills for its sanctity and power of working miracles. It was here that Rani Karnavati was saved from her enemies by god, who destroyed them in a hailstorm. Out of gratitude she built a new tower for the temple.

One of the many legends concerning Binsar states that should anyone remove anything belonging to god or his worshippers from the temple precincts, an avenging spirit pursues the culprit and compels him to restore it twenty-fold. Even the faithless and dishonest are reformed by a visit to Binsar. Hence the proverb : *Bhai, Binsar ka loha janlo samajhlo.*

It is said that although the forests in the neighbourhood abounded with tigers, not one attacked a pilgrim, owing to the protecting influence of god. Indeed, it was considered propitious to see a tiger on the way to Binsar. This belief is still held, although tigers now being less numerous, the chances of seeing one are not as good as in those days of yore.

Unusual though it was for a woman to have ruled over a large tract of hill country, there were women rulers before Karnavati in parts of western Garhwal. Huien Tsang, the seventh century traveller, in his sub-Himalayan travels speaks of a kingdom called Barhampura, later identified with Barahat in Rawain Garhwal (now Uttarkashi), which 'produced gold and where for ages a woman has been the ruler and so it is called the kingdom of a woman. The husband of the reigning woman is called king, but he knows nothing of the affairs of state. This man manages the wars and sows the land....'

There is little or no recorded history for that period, but it would appear that for a woman to have governed large tracts of land was not unusual. The sociology of the area has always been unique.

Nearer in time, I can imagine the Doon of Rani Karnavati's reign—scattered villages, a little cultivation here and there, and large tracts of forest reaching up to the foothills and beyond. Tigers and elephants roamed these forests, and so did many wild animals now extinct in the area.

Inevitably, immigration took place from other parts of the country, but even as late as 1817, when the British wrested the Doon from the Gurkhas, a population count (Walton's Gazetteer) showed Dehra Dun to have a population of two thousand and one hundred, with five hundred dwelling-places; hardly a town by today's standards.

Compare this with today's five lakhs and you have a classic example of urbanisation and population growth on an impressive scale, most of it during the last fifty years.

And yet, parts of the Doon are still lovely. Almost any tree or flower will grow in this fertile valley. Hopefully, when we go into the twenty-first century, there will still be a few gardens and open spaces for our children to enjoy.

And now that Dehra Dun is the capital of the State of Uttarakhand, all statistics need an upward revision. Never having been any good at maths, I can safely leave all calculations to the computers.

Growing up with Trees

DEHRA DUN WAS A GOOD PLACE FOR TREES, AND Grandfather's house was surrounded by several kinds—peepul, neem, mango, jack-fruit and papaya. There was also an ancient banyan tree. I grew up amongst these trees, and some of them planted by Grandfather grew with me.

There were two types of trees that were of special interest to a boy—trees that were good for climbing, and trees that provided fruit.

The jack-fruit tree was both these things. The fruit itself—the largest in the world—grew only on the trunk and main branches. I did not care much for the fruit, although cooked as a vegetable it made a good curry. But the tree was large and leafy and easy to climb. It was a very dark tree and if I hid in it, I could not be easily seen from below. In a hole in the tree-trunk I kept various banned items—a catapult, some lurid comics, and a large stock of chewing-gum. Perhaps they are still there, because I forgot to collect them when we finally went away.

The banyan tree grew behind the house. Its spreading branches, which hung to the ground and took root again, formed a number of twisting passageways and gave me endless pleasure. The tree was older than the house, older than my grandparents, as old as Dehra. I could hide myself in its branches, behind thick green leaves, and spy on the world below. I could read in it too, propped up against the bole of the tree, with Treasure Island or the Jungle Books or comics like Wizard or Hotspur which, unlike the forbidden Superman and others like him, were full of clean-cut schoolboy heroes.

The banyan tree was a world in itself, populated with small beasts and large insects. While the leaves were still pink and tender, they would be visited by the delicate map butterfly, who committed her eggs to their care. The 'honey' on the leaves—an edible smear—also attracted the little striped squirrels, who soon grew used to my presence and became quite bold. Red-headed parakeets swarmed about the tree early in the morning.

But the banyan really came to life during the monsoon, when the branches were thick with scarlet figs. These berries were not fit for human consumption, but the many birds that gathered in the tree—gossipy rosy pastors, quarrelsome mynas, cheerful bulbuls and coppersmiths, and sometimes a raucous bullying crow—feasted on them. And when night fell, and the birds were resting, the dark flying foxes flapped heavily about the tree, chewing and munching as they clambered over the branches.

Among nocturnal visitors to the jack-fruit and banyan trees was the brainfever bird, whose real name is the hawk-cuckoo. 'Brainfever, brainfever!' it seems to call, and this shrill, nagging cry will keep the soundest of sleepers awake on a hot summer night.

The British called it the brainfever bird, but there are other names for it. The Mahrattas called it 'Paos-ala' which means 'Rain is coming!' Perhaps Grandfather's interpretation of its call was the best. According to him, when the bird was tuning up for its main concert, it seemed to say: 'Oh dear, oh dear! How very hot it's getting! we feel it...WE FEEL IT...WE FEEL IT!'

Yes, the banyan tree was a noisy place during the rains. If the brainfever bird made music by night, the crickets and cicadas orchestrated during the day. As musicians, the cicadas were in a class by themselves. All through the hot weather their chorus rang through the garden, while a shower of rain, far from damping their spirits, only roused them to a greater vocal effort.

The tree-crickets were a band of willing artistes who commenced their performance at almost any time of the day, but preferably in the evenings. Delicate pale green creatures with transparent green wings, they were hard to find amongst the lush monsoon foliage; but once located, a tap on the leaf or bush on which they sat would put an immediate end to the performance.

At the height of the monsoon, the banyan tree was like an orchestra-pit with the musicians constantly turning up. Birds, insects and squirrels expressed their joy at the end of the hot weather and the cool quenching relief of the rains.

A flute in my hands, I would try adding my shrill piping to theirs. But they thought poorly of my musical ability, for whenever I played on the flute, the birds and insects would subside into a pained and puzzled silence.

A Village in Garhwal

I AWAKE TO WHAT SOUNDS LIKE THE DIN OF A FACTORY buzzer, but is in fact the music of a single vociferous cicada in the lime tree near my window.

Through the open window, I focus on a pattern of small, glossy lime leaves; then through them I see the mountains, the furthest Himalayas, striding away into an immensity of sky.

'In a thousand ages of the gods I could not tell thee of the glories of Himachal.' So confessed a Sanskrit poet at the dawn of Indian history. The sea has had Stevenson and Conrad, Melville and Hemingway, but the mountains have continued to defy the written word. We have climbed their highest peaks and crossed their most difficult passes, but still they keep their secrecy and reserve, remaining remote, mysterious and spirit-haunted.

No wonder, then, that the people who live on the mountain slopes in the mistfilled valleys of the Garhwal

Himalayas have long since learned humility and patience. Deep in the crouching mist lie their villages, while climbing the mountain slopes are forests of rhododendron, pine and deodar, soughing in the wind from the icebound passes. Pale women plough, while their men go down to the plains in search of work, for little grows on the beautiful mountains.

When I think of Manjari village in Garhwal, I see a small river, a tributary of the Ganga, rushing along the bottom of a steep, rocky valley. On the banks of the river and on the terraced hill above are small-fields of corn, barley, mustard, potatoes and onions. A few fruit trees, mostly apricot and peach, grow near the village. Some hillsides are rugged and bare, masses of quartz or granite. On hills exposed to the wind, only grass and small shrubs are able to obtain a foothold.

This landscape is typical of Garhwal, one of India's most northerly regions, with its massive snow ranges bordering on Tibet. Although thinly populated, Garhwal does not provide much of a living for its people.

'You have such beautiful scenery,' I said, after crossing the first range of hills.

'True,' said my friend, 'but we cannot eat the scenery.'

Any yet these are cheerful sturdy people, with great powers of endurance. Somehow they manage to wrest a precarious living from the unhelpful, calcinated soil.

I am their guest for a few days. My friend Gajadhar has brought me home to his village above the Nayar river. My

A Village in Garhwal

own home is in the hill-station of Mussoorie, two day's journey to the west. We took a train across the Ganga and into the foothills, and then a bus—no, several buses—and finally, made dizzy by fast driving around hairpin bends, alighted at the small hill-town of Lansdowne, chief recruiting centre for the Garhwal Rifles. Garhwal soldiers distinguished themselves fighting alongside British troops in both the World Wars, and they still form a high percentage of recruits to the Indian Army. The money orders they send home are the mainstay of the village economy.

Lansdowne is just over 6,000 ft in altitude. From there we walked some twenty-five miles between sunrise and sunset, until we came to Manjari village clinging to the terraced slopes of the Dhudatoli range.

And this is my fourth morning in the village. Other mornings I woke to the throaty chuckles of the red-billed blue magpies, as they glided between oak tree and medlar, but today the cicada has drowned all birdsong. It is a little out of season for the cicadas, but perhaps the sudden warm spell in late September has deceived them into thinking it is again the mating season.

As usual, I am the last to get up. Gajadhar is exercising in the courtyard, going through an odd combination of Yoga and Swedish exercises. With his sturdy physique and quick intelligence, I am sure he will realise his ambition of joining the Indian Army as an officer-cadet. He is proud of his family's army tradition, as indeed are most Garhwalis who remember that the first Indian to win the Victoria Cross (in World War I) was a Garhwali Rifleman Gabbar Singh Negi, who lost his life in the muddy fields of Flanders.

Gajadhar's younger brother Chakradhar, who is slim and fair with high cheek-bones, is milking the family's buffalo. Normally he would be on his long walk to school, which is five miles away, but this being a holiday, he is able to stay home and help with the household chores.

His mother is lighting a fire. She is a handsome woman, even though her ears, weighed down by heavy silver ear-rings, have lost their natural shape. Garhwali women

usually invest their savings in silver and gold ornaments—
nose-rings, earrings, bangles and bracelets, and sometimes
necklaces of old silver rupees. At the time of marriage, it is
usually the boy's parents who make a gift of land to the
parents of an attractive girl, a sort of dowry system in
reverse.

This boy's father is a corporal in the army and is away
for most of the year. When Gajadhar marries, his wife will
most likely stay in the village with his mother to help look
after the fields, house, goats and buffalo. Gajadhar will see
her only when he comes home on leave.

The village is far above the river and most of the fields
depend on rainfall. But water must be fetched for cooking,

A Hill Village—Garhwal

washing and drinking. So, after a breakfast of hot milk and thick chapatties stuffed with minced radish, the brother and I set off down the rough track to the river.

The sun has climbed the mountains, but it has yet to reach the narrow valley. We bathe in the river, the brothers diving in off a massive rock; but I wade in circumspectly, unfamiliar with the river's depths and currents. The water, a milky blue, has come from the melting snows and is very cold. I bathe quickly and then make a dash for a strip of sand where a little sunshine has split down the hillside in warm, golden pools of light. At the same time the song of the whistling-thrush emerges like a dark secret from the wooded shadows.

The Manjari school is only up to class five and has about forty pupils. And if these children (mostly boys) would like to continue their schooling, then, like Chakradhar, they must walk the five miles to the high school in the next big village.

'Don't you get tired walking ten miles every day?' I asked him.

'I am used to it,' says Chakradhar. And I like walking.'

I know that he has only two meals a day—one at seven in the morning when he leaves home, and the other at six or seven in the evening when he returns from school. I ask him if he gets hungry on the way.

'There is always some wild fruit,' he says.

He is an expert on wild fruit: the purple berries of the thorny kingora (barberry) ripening in May and June; wild strawberries like drops of blood on the dark green monsoon grass; sour cherries, wild pears and raspberries. Chakradhar's strong teeth and probing tongue extract whatever tang or sweetness lies hidden in them. In the spring there are the rhododendron flowers. His mother makes them into jam, but Chakradhar likes them as they are. He places the petals on his tongue and chews till the sweet juice trickles down his throat. He has never been ill.

'But what happens when someone is ill?' I ask, knowing that in the village there are no medicines, no hospital.

'He rests until he feels better.' says Gajadhar. 'We have a few remedies. But if someone is very sick, we carry him to the hospital at Lansdowne.'

Fortunately the clear mountain air and simple diet keep the people of this area free from most illness. The greatest dangers come from unexpected disasters, such as an accident with an axe or scythe or an attack by a wild animal such as a bear.

I am woken one night by a rumbling and thumping on the roof. I wake Gajadhar and ask him what is happening.

'It's only a bear,' he says.

'Is it trying to get in?'

'No. It's been in the cornfield and now it's after the pumpkins on the roof.'

At the approach of winter, when snow covers the higher mountains, the brown and black Himalayan bears descend to lower altitudes in search of food. Being short-sighted and suspicious of anything that moves, they can be dangerous;

but like most wild animals they avoid humans when they can and are aggressive only when accompanied by their cubs.

Gajadhar advises me to run downhill if chased by a bear. Bears, he says, find it easier to run uphill than downhill!

The idea of being chased by a bear does not appeal to me, but the following night I stay up with him to try and prevent the bear from depleting his cornfield. We take up our position on a high promontory of rock, which gives us a clear view of the moonlit field.

A little after midnight, the bear comes down to the edge of the field. Standing up as high as possible on his hind legs, and peering about to see if the field is empty, he comes cautiously out of the forest and makes his way towards the corn.

Suddenly he stops, his attention caught by some Buddhist prayer-flags which have been strung up recently by a band of wandering Tibetans. Noticing the flags, he gives a little grunt of disapproval and begins to move back into the forest. But then, being one of the most inquisitive animals, he advances again and stands on his hind legs looking at the flags, first at one side and then at the other.

Finding that the flags do not attack him, the bear moves confidently up to them and tears them all down.

After making a careful examination of the flags, he moves into the field.

This is when Gajadhar starts shouting. The rest of the village wakes up and people come out of their houses beating drums and empty kerosene-oil tins.

Deprived of his dinner, the bear takes off in a bad temper. He runs downhill, and at a good speed too; and I am glad that I am not in his way just then. Uphill or downhill, an angry bear is best given a very wide berth.

For Gajadhar, impatient to know the result of his army entrance exam, the following day is a test of patience.

The postman has yet to arrive. The mail is brought in relays from Lansdowne, and the Manjari postman, who has to deliver letters at several small villages enroute, should arrive around noon, but now it is three in the afternoon.

First we hear that there has been a landslide and that the postman cannot reach us. Then we hear that although there had been a landslide, the postman passed the spot in safety. Another alarming rumour has it that the postman disappeared with the landslide. This is soon denied. The postman is safe. It is only the mailbag that has disappeared.

Anyway, he is soon forgiven (and given another heavy meal), because Gajadhar has passed his exam and will leave with me in the morning.

His mother insists on celebrating her son's success by feasting her friends and neighbour. There is a partridge (a present from a neighbour who conjectures that Gajadhar will make a fine husband for his daughter), and three chickens: rich fare for folk whose normal diet consists mostly of lentils, rice, potatoes and onions.

After dinner there are songs, and Gajadhar's mother sings of the homesickness of those who are separated from their loved ones and their homes in the hills. It is an old Garhwali folk-song:

Oh mountain swift, you are from my father's home—
Speak, oh speak, in the courtyard of my parents,
My mother will hear you.
She will send my brother to fetch me.
A grain of rice alone in the cooking-pot
Cries, 'I wish I could get out!'
Likewise I wonder—
Will I ever reach my father's house?

The hookah is passed round, and stories are told, gossip exchanged. It is almost midnight when the last guest leaves. Chakradhar approaches me as I am about to retire for the night.

'Will you come again?' he asks.

'I'm sure I will,' I reply. 'If not next year, then the year after'.

The moon has not yet come up. Lanterns swing in the dark. Almost everyone, including the blind man, carries a lantern. And if you ask the blind man what he needs a lantern for, he will reply: 'So that fools do not stumble against me in the dark.'

The lanterns flit silently over the hillside and go out one by one. This Garhwali day, which is just like any other day in the hills, slips quietly into the silence of the mountains.

I stretch myself out on my cot. Outside the small window, the sky is brilliant with stars. As I close my eyes, someone brushes against the lime tree, bruising its leaves; and the good fresh fragrance comes to me on the night air, making the moment memorable for all time.

Tales of Old Mussoorie

AT ONE TIME VISITORS TO MUSSOORIE FREQUENTLY FOUND themselves persuaded to climb to the top of a local peak called 'Gun Hill', from which one is able to obtain a view of the greater Himalayas. Today a cable-car takes tourists to the top of the hill, from which, besides the snows, Mussoorie waterworks, too, can be seen, but of a 'gun' there is no sign and they may be pardoned for wondering how the hill acquired its impressive name. We hope to enlighten them on this, and other aspects, of the hill-station's distant though not ancient past.

Before 1919, noon-time was indicated by the firing of a cannon from the top of 'Gun Hill', possibly because cannons were cheaper than clocks in those days. At first the gun faced east; then soon after its installation, a complaint came from the Grey Castle Nursing Home that the gun when fired 'often let loose piaster from the ceiling of the wards, which fell on patients' beds and unnerved them'. It could not be pointed north because it would then have blasted away a house called 'Dilkush'; so it was faced north-east, but that again couldn't be made its permanent position, for the Crystal Bank then complained. Turned to the south, it almost succeeded in fulfilling its legitimate duty, but that was before the gunner forgot to remove the ramrod from the barrel; and on booming noon to the populace, the cannon sent the ramrod clean through the roof of the Savoy hotel.

Public opinion consequently was mounting against the gun, and it was turned around once more to face the Mall. The boom was usually produced by ramming down the barrel a mixture of moist grass and cotton waste, after the powder was in place. Due to an accidental overcharge of powder, one of these cannon-balls landed with some force right in the lap of a lady who was being taken along the Mall in a rickshaw. It was the last straw or, to be exact, the last cannon-ball, for the gun was dismantled soon after the incident.

A peep into the life of the hill-station before the turn of the century is a fascinating exercise; but before giving the reader further anecdotes, we should fill in the background with a brief historical sketch of the hill-station.

In the year 1825, the Superintendent of the Doon was a certain Mr Shore, who occasionally found time from his official duties to scramble up the range, then known as 'Mansuri' because of the prevalence of a shrub known in the vernacular as the Mansur plant. He found that the range had a number of 'flats', some of which accommodated the huts of cowherds who grazed their cattle on them during the summer months. The hills were then well forested and game plentiful; so the first construction was a shooting-box built jointly by Mr Shore and Captain Young of the Sirmur Rifles. It has long since disappeared, but is said to have been located on the Camel's Back, facing north. The first home—still recognisable—was 'Mullingar' in Landour, built in 1826 by Captain Young. Landour soon became a convalescent depot for British troops; the old convalescent hospital now forms the nucleus of the offices of the Defence Institute of Work Study. Soon civilians were flocking to Mussoorie, building houses as far apart as 'Cloud End' to the west and 'Dahlia Bank' to the east, separated by some twelve miles. In 1832, Colonel Everest (after whom the mountain is named) as Surveyor-General opened his Survey of India office in 'The Park' and made a road to it.

People came to Mussoorie for health, business and pleasure; and amongst the pleasure-seekers we find the Hon'ble Emily Eden, sister of Lord George Eden, Earl of Auckland, Governor General of India. One of our earliest visitors, she records in her famous diaries that 'in the afternoon we took a beautiful ride up to Landour, but the paths are very narrow on that side, and our courage somehow oozed out, and first we came to a place where they said, "This was where poor Major Blundell and his pony fell over and they were both dashed to atoms," and then there was a board stuck in a tree, "From this spot a private in the Cameroons fell and was killed......" We had to get off our ponies and lead them, and altogether I thought much of poor Major Blundell. It is impossible to imagine more beautiful scenery'.

Though there were no proper roads in Mussoorie in those early days, some of the cliff-edge accidents were undoubtedly caused by the beer that was then so cheap and plentiful in the hill-station.

Mr Bohle, one of the pioneers of brewing in India, started the 'Old Brewery' near Hathipaon in 1830. Two years later he got into trouble for supplying beer to soldiers who were alleged to have presented forged passes. Mr Bohle was called to account by Captain (by now Colonel) Young for distilling spirits without a license, and had to close his concern. Undaunted, he was back in 1834, building 'Bohle's Brewery', and became a popular figure in Mussoorie society. His tomb in the Camel's Back cemetery is still one of the most impressive.

Scandal again erupted in the brewery business in 1876, when everyone suddenly started talking of a much improved brew. It came from Vat 42 in Whymer and Company's 'Crown Brewery'. The beer was retasted until the diminishing level of the barrel revealed the perfectly brewed remains of a human! Someone had fallen into the vat and been drowned, and, all unknown to himself, had given the beer-trade a real fillip. The author of *A Mussoorie Miscellany* (H.C. Williams) informs us that 'meat was thereafter recognised as the missing component and scrupulosuly added till more modern, and less cannibalistic, means were discovered to satiate the froth-blower'.

A bold, bad place was Mussoorie in those days, according to the correspondent of the *Statesman,* who, in his paper of 22nd October 1884, wrote 'Ladies and gentlemen, after attending church, proceeded to a drinking shop, a restaurant adjoining the library, and there indulged freely in pegs, not one but many; and at a Fancy Bazaar held this season, a lady stood up on her chair and offered her kisses to gentlemen at Rs 5 each. What would they think of such a state of society at home?'

Fifty years later, a Mussoorie lady auctioned a single kiss for Rs 300. A vivid illustration of the inflationary process throughout history.

But inspite of such goings-on, or perhaps because of them, the inhabitants were conscious of their spiritual needs, and a number of churches were soon dotted about the hill-station, the oldest of them being Christ Church (1836).

When, in March 1905, Her Royal Highness the Princess of Wales (later Queen Mary) visited Mussoorie, she planted a deodar tree outside Christ Church. The plaque commemorating this event can still be seen, now almost embedded in the trunk of the tree.

Some thirty years later, the chaplain of Christ Church was the fair-minded Reverend T.W. Chisolm. In his usual Sunday service prayers, in the year 1933, he sought god's help for veteran Indian leader and freedom-fighter, Pandit Motilal Nehru, a regular visitor to Mussoorie, who was then seriously ill. There was an immediate hullaballoo in all official tea sessions, and the chaplain was reprimanded. This caused him to comment, 'that in these years of our Lord, Holy Orders can be interpreted to mean wholly Government orders.'

It is easy enough to get to Mussoorie today, but how did visitors manage it before the advent of the railway and the motorcar? It was surely a difficult exercise. Mr Shore and Captain Young merely scrambled up the goat tracks to get here; and Lady Eden used her pony to canter along paths and 'up precipices'; but before that, one detrained at Ghaziabad (near Delhi), engaged a bullock-cart or tonga, and then proceeded in the direction of the Himalayas as speedily as only a bullock-cart or tonga could go. After that, one either walked, rode a pony, or was carried uphill in a doolie, a crude sort of palanquin.

By the turn of the century, the 'Sind, Punjab and Delhi Railway' had got as far as Saharanpur, and the bullock-cart had given way to the dak-ghari.

The only way to reach Dehra Dun, en route to Mussoorie, was by the dak-ghari or 'night-mail'.

Dak-Ghari ponies were different animals, 'always attempting to turn around and get into carriage with the passengers,' as one disgruntled traveller described them. It was only when the coachman used his whip liberally and reviled the ponies' ancestors as far back as three or four generations that the beasts could be persuaded to move. And once they started, there was no stopping them; it was a gallop all the way to the first stage, where the ponies were changed to the accompaniment of a bugle blown by the coachman in true Dickensian fashion.

The journey through the Siwaliks really began—as it still does—at the Mohand Pass. The ascent starts with a gradual gradient, which increases as the road becomes more steep and winding. The hills are abrupt and perpendicular on the southern side, but slope gently away to the north.

At this stage of the journey, drums were beaten (if it was daytime) and torches were lit (if it was night), because frequently wild elephants resented the approach of the dak-ghari and, trumpeting a challenge, would throw the ponies into panic and confusion and send them racing back to the plains.

The railway reached Dehra Dun in 1901. Till then the main overnight stop was at Rajpur, and the well-known hostelries and forwarding agencies at Rajpur were the 'Ellenborough Hotel', the 'Prince of Wales Hotel', and the 'Agency Retiring Rooms' of Messrs Buckle and Company's 'Bullock Train Agency'. They have long since disappeared. As Dehra Dun grew in importance, Rajpur's importance dwindled, and for many years its long winding bazaar resembled a ghost-town.

Soon the Savoy and Charleville Hotels opened. Massive furniture, grand-pianos, billiard-tables, barrels of cider and crates of champagne had all come up the hill in lumbering bullock-carts. In 1909, the hotels were suddenly ablaze with light, for this was the year when electricity came to Mussoorie. Before that, the ballrooms and dining-rooms had been hung with chandeliers, the rooms lit by candlelight, and the kitchens with spirit-lamps.

It was after World War I in the 'gay twenties' that the Charleville and the Savoy entered the most popular era, when they were to be as well-known as Raffles in Singapore or the Imperial in Tokyo. Wealthy Indian princes and their families and staff occupied entire wings of the Savoy Hotel. The Savoy Orchestra played every night, and the ballroom was full of couples doing the tango or fox-trot, the latest dancing craze of those days.

After India's Independence in 1947, Mussoorie went through a difficult period. The British had gone, and the wealthy princes and landowners were also finding times difficult. Hotels and boarding-houses began to close down. Then, in the early sixties, the prosperous Indian middle-classes became hill-station conscious, and once again crowds thronged the Mall on summer evenings. These days the foreign tourist is discovering the delights of the lower Himalayas.

Those who wish to move further into the mountains, either on foot or by road, have a wealth of flora and fauna to discover and enjoy. One of the remarkable features of the Himalayas is the abruptness with which they rise from the plains, and this gives them a verdure that is totally different from that of the plains.

None of the common trees of the plains are to be found in the hills. At elevations of 4,000 ft, the long-leaved pine appears. From 5,000 ft there are several kinds of evergreen oak, and above 6,000 ft you find rhododendron, deodar, maple, the hill crypress, and the beautiful horse-chestnut. Still higher up, the silver fir is common; but at 12,000 ft the firs become stunted and dwarfed, and the birch and juniper replace them. At this height raspberries grow wild, amongst yellow colt's-foot dandelion, blue gentian, purple columbine, anemone and edelweiss.

Not every hillside is covered with foliage. Many hills are bare and rugged, too precipitous for cultivation. Sometimes they are masses of quartz, limestone or granite.

Just as the trees of the plains differ from those of the hills, so do the animals and birds. The bear, the goral (a goat-like animal), the marten, the civet-cat, the snow leopard, and the musk-deer, all belong to the Himalayas. The caw of the house-crow is replaced by the deeper note of the corby, and the melodious green hill-pigeon takes the place of the small brown dove.

You do not always see the birds, but you can hear them. As you trek in the interior, or wander along a quiet road in the hill-station, the sound of birds is very pleasant to hear; just as the sound of water in the valleys, the singing of the hill people, the smell of the pines, and the blue smoke rising from the villages, are always with you in the Himalayas.

Landour Bazaar

IN MOST NORTH INDIAN BAZAARS, THERE IS A CLOCK TOWER. And like most clocks in clock towers, this one works in fits and starts: listless in summer, sluggish during the monsoon, stopping altogether when it snows in January. Almost every year the tall brick structure gets a coat of paint. It was pink last year. Now it's a livid purple.

From the clock tower, at one end, to the mule sheds at the other, this old Mussoorie bazaar is a mile long. The tall, shaky three-storey buildings cling to the mountainside, shutting out the sunlight. They are even shakier now that heavy trucks have started rumbling down the narrow street, originally made for nothing heavier than a rickshaw. The street is narrow and damp, retaining all the bazaar smells—sweetmeats frying, smoke from wood or charcoal fires, the sweat and urine of mules, petrol fumes, all these mingle with the smell of mist and old buildings and distant pines.

The bazaar sprang up about a hundred and fifty years ago to serve the needs of British soldiers, who were sent to the Landour convalescent depot to recover from sickness or wounds. The old military hospital, built in 1827, now houses the Defence Institute of Work Study.* One old resident of the bazaar, a ninety-year-old tailor, can remember the time, in the early years of the century, when the Redcoats marched through the small bazaar on their way to the cantonment church. And they always carried their rifles into church, remembering how many had been surprised in churches during the 1857 uprising.

Today, the Landour bazaar serves the local population, Mussoorie itself being more geared to the needs and interest of tourists. There are a number of silversmiths in Landour. They fashion silver nose-rings, earrings, bracelets and anklets, which are bought by the women from the surrounding Jaunpuri villages. One silversmith had a chest full of old silver rupees. These rupees are sometimes hung on thin silver chains and worn as pendants. I have often seen women in Garhwal wearing pendants or necklaces of rupees embossed with the profiles of Queen Victoria or King Edward VII.

At the other extreme there are the kabari shops, where you can pick up almost everything—a taperecorder discarded by a Woodstock student, or a piece of furniture

---

*The Defence Institute of Work Study has been renamed the Institute of Technologic Management.

from Grandmother's time in the hill-station. Old clothes, Victorian bric-a-brac, and bits of modern gadgetry vie for your attention.

The old clothes are often more reliable than the new. Last winter I bought a new pullover marked 'Made in Nepal' from a Tibetan pavement vendor. I was wearing it on the way home when it began to rain. By the time I reached my cottage, the pullover had shrunk inches and I had some difficulty getting out of it! It was now just the right size for Bijju, the milkman's twelve-year-old son, and I gave it to the boy. But it continued to shrink at every wash, and it is now being worn by Teju, Bijju's younger brother, who is eight.

At the dark windy corner in the bazaar, one always found an old man hunched up over his charcoal fire, roasting peanuts. He'd been there for as long as I could remember, and he could be seen at almost any hour of the day or night, in all weathers.

He was probably quite tall, but I never saw him standing up. One judged his height from his long, loose limbs. He was very thin, probably tubercular, and the high cheekbones added to the tautness of his tightly stretched skin.

His peanuts were always fresh, crisp and hot. They were popular with small boys, who had a few coins to spend on their way to and from school. On cold winter evenings, there was always a demand for peanuts from people of all ages.

No one seemed to know the old man's name. No one had ever thought of asking. One just took his presence for granted. He was as fixed a landmark as the clock tower or the old cherry tree that grew crookedly from the hillside. He seemed less perishable than the tree, more dependable than the clock. He had no family, but in a way all the world was his family because he was in continuous contact with people. And yet he was a remote sort of being; always polite, even to children, but never familiar. He was seldom alone, but he must have been lonely.

Summer nights he rolled himself up in a thin blanket and slept on the ground beside the dying embers of his fire. During winter he waited until the last cinema show was over, before retiring to the rickshaw coolies' shelter where there was protection from the freezing wind.

Did he enjoy being alive? I often wondered. He was not a joyful person; but then neither was he miserable. Perhaps he was one of those who do not attach overmuch importance to themselves, who are emotionally uninvolved in the life around them, content with their limitations, their dark corners; people on whom cares rest lightly, simply because they do not care at all.

I wanted to get to know the old man better, to sound him out on the immense questions involved in roasting peanuts all one's life; but it's too late now. He died last summer.

That corner remained very empty, very dark, and every time I passed it, I was haunted by visions of the old peanut vendor, troubled by the questions I did not ask; and I wondered if he was really as indifferent to life as he appeared to be.

Then, a few weeks ago, there was a new occupant of the corner, a new seller of peanuts. No relative of the old man, but a boy of thirteen or fourteen. The human personality can impose its own nature on its surroundings. In the old man's time it seemed a dark, gloomy corner. Now it's lit up by sunshine—a sunny personality, smiling, chattering. Old age gives way to youth; and I'm glad I won't be alive when the new peanut vendor grows old. One shouldn't see too many people grow old.

Leaving the main bazaar behind, I walk some way down the Mussoorie-Tehri road, a fine road to walk on, in spite of the dust from an occasional bus or jeep. From Mussoorie to Chamba, a distance of some thirty-five miles, the road seldom descends below 7,000 ft, and there is a continual vista of the snow ranges to the north and valleys and rivers to the south. Dhanaulti is one of the lovelier spots, and the Garhwal Mandal Vikas Nigam has a rest house here, where one can spend an idyllic weekend. Some years ago I walked all the way to Chamba, spending the night at Kaddukhal, from where a short climb takes one to the Surkhanda Devi temple.

Leaving the Tehri Road, one can also trek down to the little Aglar river and then up to Nag Tibba, 9,000 ft, which has good oak forests and animals ranging from barking-deer to Himalayan bear; but this is an arduous trek and you must be prepared to spend the night in the open or seek the hospitality of a village.

On this particular day I reach Suakholi and rest in a tea-shop, a loose stone structure with a tin roof held down by stones. It serves the bus passengers, mule drivers, milkmen, and others who use this road.

I find a couple of mules tethered to a pine tree. The mule drivers, handsome men in tattered clothes, sit on a bench in the shade of the tree, drinking tea from brass tumblers. The shopkeeper, a man of indeterminate age— the cold dry winds from the mountain passes having crinkled his face like a walnut—greets me enthusiastically, as he always does. He even produces a chair, which looks a survivor from one of Wilson's rest houses, and may even be a Sheraton. Fortunately the Mussoorie kabaris do not know about it or they'd have snapped it up long ago. In any case, the stuffing has come out of the seat. The shopkeeper apologises for its condition: 'The rats were nesting in it.' And then, to reassure me: 'But they have gone now.'

I would just as soon be on the bench with the Jaunpuri mule drivers, but I do not wish to offend Mela Ram, the tea-shop owner; so I take his chair into the shade and lower myself into it.

'How long have you kept this shop?'

'Oh, ten, fifteen years, I do not remember.'

He hasn't bothered to count the years. Why should he? Outside the towns in the isolation of the hills, life is simply a matter of yesterday, today and tomorrow. And not always tomorrow.

Unlike Mela Ram, the mule drivers have somewhere to go and something to deliver—sacks of potatoes! From Jaunpur to Jaunsar, the potato is probably the crop best suited to these stony, terraced fields. They have to deliver their potatoes in Landour Bazaar and return to their village before nightfall; and soon they lead their pack animals away, along the dusty road to Mussoorie.

'Tea or lassi?' Mela Ram offers me a choice, and I choose the curd preparation, which is sharp, sour and very refreshing. The wind soughs gently in the upper branches of the pine trees, and I relax in my Sheraton chair like some eighteenth century Nawab who has brought his own furniture into the wilderness. I can see why Wilson did not want to return to the plains when he came his way in the 1850s. Instead he went further and higher into the mountains and made his home among the people of the Bhagirathi valley.

Having wandered some way down the Tehri road, it is quite late by the time I return to the Landour bazaar. Lights still twinkle on the hills, but shop fronts are shuttered and the little bazaar is silent. The people living on either side of the narrow street can hear my footsteps, and I hear their casual remarks, music, a burst of laughter.

Through a gap in the rows of buildings I can see Pari Tibba outlined in the moonlight. A greenish phosphorescent glow appears to move here and there about the hillside. This is the 'fairy light' that gives the hill its name Pari Tibba, Fairy Hill. I have no explanation for it, and I don't know anyone else who has been able to explain it satisfactorily; but often from my window I see this greenish light zigzagging about the hill.

A three-quarter moon is up, and the tin roofs of the bazaar, drenched with dew, glisten in the moonlight. Although the street is unlit, I need no torch. I can see every step of the way. I can even read the headlines on the discarded newspaper lying in the gutter.

Although I am alone on the road, I am aware of the life pulsating around me. It is a cold night, doors and windows are shut; but through the many clinks, narrow fingers of light reach out into the night. Who could still be up? A shopkeeper going through his accounts, a college student preparing for his exams, someone coughing and groaning in the dark.

Three stray dogs are romping in the middle of the road. It is their road now, and they abandon themselves to a wild chase, almost knocking me down.

A jackal slinks across the road, looking to the right and left—he knows his road-drill—to make sure the dogs have gone. A field rat wriggles through a hole in a rotting plank on its nightly foray among sacks of grain and pulses.

Yes, this is an old bazaar. The bakers, tailors, silversmiths, and wholesale merchants are the grandsons of those who followed the mad sahibs to this hilltop in the thirties and forties of the last century. Most of them are plainsmen, quite prosperous, even though many of their houses are crooked and shaky.

Although the shopkeepers and tradesmen are fairly prosperous, the hill people—those who come from the surrounding Tehri and Jaunpur villages—are usually poor. Their small holdings and rocky fields do not provide them with much of a living, and men and boys have to often come into the hill-station or go down to the cities in search of a livelihood. They pull rickshaws, or work in hotels and restaurants. Most of them have somewhere to stay.

But as I pass along the deserted street under the shadow of the clock tower, I find a boy huddled in a recess, a thin shawl wrapped around his shoulders. He is wide awake and shivering.

I pass by, my head down, my thoughts already on the warmth of my small cottage only a mile away. And then I stop. It is almost as though the bright moonlight has stopped me, holding my shadow in thrall.

'If I am not for myself,
who will be for me?
And if I am not for others,
what am I?
And if not now, when?'

The words of an ancient sage beat upon my mind. I walk back to the shadows where the boy crouches. He does not say anything, but he looks up at me, puzzled and apprehensive. All the warnings of well-wishers crowd in upon me—stories of crime by night, of assault and robber, 'ill met by moonlight'.

But this is not northern Ireland or Lebanon or the streets of New York. This is Landour in the Garhwal Himalayas. And the boy is no criminal. I can tell from his features that he comes from the hills beyond Tehri. He has come here looking for work and has yet to find any.

'Have you somewhere to stay?' I asked.

He shakes his head; but something about my tone of voice has given him confidence, because now there is a glimmer of hope, a friendly appeal in his eyes.

I have committed myself. I cannot pass on. A shelter for the night—that's the very least one human should be able to expect from another.

'If you can walk some way,' I offer, 'I can give you a bed and blanket.'

He gets up immediately, a thin boy, wearing only a shirt and part of an old track-suit. He follows me without any hesitation. I cannot now betray his trust. Nor can I fail to trust him.

Along the Mandakini

TO SEE A RIVER FOR THE FIRST TIME AT ITS CONFLUENCE with another great river is, for me, a special moment in time. And so it was at Rudraprayag, where the waters of the Mandakini joined with the waters of the Alaknanda, the one having come from the glacial snows above Kedarnath, the other from the Himalayan heights beyond Badrinath. Both sacred rivers, both destined to become the holy Ganga further downstream.

I fell in love with the Mandakini at first sight. Or was it the valley that I fell in love with? I am not sure, and it doesn't really matter. The valley is the river.

While the Alaknanda valley, especially in its higher reaches, is a deep and narrow gorge where precipitous outcrops of rock hang threateningly over the traveller, the Mandakini valley is broader, gentler, the terraced fields wider, the banks of the river a green sward in many places.

Somehow, one does not feel that one is at the mercy of the Mandakini, whereas one is always at the mercy of the Alaknanda with its sudden landslips and floods.

Rudraprayag is hot. It is probably a pleasant spot in winter, but at the end of June it is decidedly hot. Perhaps its chief claim to fame is that it gave its name to the dreaded man-eating leopard of Rudraprayag who, in the course of seven years (1918-25), accounted for more than three hundred victims. It was finally shot by the fifty-one-year-old Jim Corbett, who recounted the saga of his long hunt for the killer in his fine book, *The Man-Eating Leopard of Rudraprayag.*

The place at which the leopard was shot was the village of Gulabrai, two miles south of Rudraprayag. Under a large mango tree stands a memorial raised to Jim Corbett by officers and men of the Border Roads Organisation. It is a happy gesture to one who loved Garhwal and India. Unfortunately several buffaloes are tethered close by, and one has to wade through slush and buffalo dung to get to the memorial-stone. A board tacked on to the mango tree attracts the attention of motorists, who might pass without noticing the memorial which is off to one side.

The killer leopard was noted for its direct method of attack on humans; and in spite of being poisoned, trapped in a cave, and shot at innumerable times, it did not lose its contempt for man. Two English sportsmen, covering both ends of the old suspension bridge over the Alaknanda, fired several times at the man-eater but to little effect.

It was not long before the leopard acquired a reputation among the hill folk for being an evil spirit. A Sadhu was suspected of turning into the leopard by night, and was only saved from being lynched by the ingenuity of Philip Mason, then Deputy Commissioner of Garhwal. Mason kept the Sadhu in custody until the leopard made his next attack, thus proving the man innocent. Years later, when Mason turned novelist and (using the pen name Philip Woodruffe) wrote *The Wild Sweet Witch*, he had as a character a beautiful young woman who turns into a man-eating leopard by night.

Corbett's host at Gulabrai was one of the few who survived an encounter with the leopard. It left him with a hole in his throat. Apart from being a superb story-teller, Corbett displayed great compassion for people from all walks of life and is still a legend in Garhwal and Kumaon amongst people who have never read his books.

In June one does not linger long in the steamy heat of Rudraprayag. But as one travels up the river, making a gradual ascent of the Mandakini valley, there is a cool breeze coming down from the snows, and the smell of rain is in the air.

The thriving little township of Agastmuni spreads itself along the wide river banks, and further upstream, near a little place called Chandrapuri, we cannot resist breaking our journey to sprawl on the tender green grass that slopes gently down to the swift flowing river. A small rest house is in the making. Around it, banana fronds sway and poplar leaves dance in the breeze.

This is no sluggish river of the plains, but a fast-moving current tumbling over rocks, turning and twisting in its efforts to discover the easiest way for its frothy snow-fed waters to escape the mountains. Escape is the word, for the constant plaint of many a Garhwali is that, while his hills abound in rivers, the water runs down and away and little, if any, reaches the fields and villages above it. Cultivation must depend on the rain and not on the river.

The road climbs gradually, still keeping to the river. Just outside Guptakashi, my attention is drawn to a clump of huge trees sheltering a small but ancient temple. We stop here and enter the shade of the trees.

The temple is deserted. It is a temple dedicated to Shiva, and in the courtyard are several river-rounded stone lingams on which leaves and blossoms have fallen. No one seems to come here, which is strange, since it is on the pilgrim route. Two boys from a neighbouring field leave their yoked bullocks to come and talk to me, but they cannot tell me much about the temple except to confirm that it is seldom visited. The buses do not stop here.' That seems explanation enough. For where the buses go, the pilgrims go; and where the pilgrims go, other pilgrims will follow. Thus far and no further.

The trees seem to be magnolias. But I have never seen magnolia trees grow to such huge proportions. Perhaps they are something else. Never mind; let them remain a sweet-scented mystery.

Guptakashi in the evening is all abustle. A coachload of pilgrims (headed for Kedarnath) has just arrived, and the tea-shops near the bus-stand are doing brisk business. Then the 'local' bus from Ukhimath, across the river, arrives and many of the passengers head for a tea-shop famed for its samosas. The local bus is called the Bhook-Hartal, the 'Hunger-strike' bus.

'How did it get that name?' I asked one of the samosa-eaters.

'Well, it's an interesting story. For a long time we had been asking the authorities to provide a bus service for the local people and for the villagers who live off the roads. All the buses came from Srinagar or Rishikesh and were taken up by pilgrims. The locals could't find room on them. But our pleas went unheard until the whole town, or most of it, anyway decided to go on hunger-strike. That worked! And so the bus is named after our successful hunger-strike.'

They nearly put me out of business too,' said the tea-shop owner cheerfully 'Nobody ate any samosas for two days!'

There is no cinema or public place of entertainment at Guptakashi, and the town goes to sleep early and wakes early.

At six, the hillside, green from recent rain, sparkles in the morning sunshine. The snow-capped Chaukhamba (7140 metres) is dazzling. The air is clear; no smoke or dust up here. The climate, I am told, is mild all the year round, judging by the scent and shape of the flowers, and the

boys call them Champa (Hindi for magnolia blossom).
Ukhimath, on the other side of the river, lies in the shadow.
It gets the sun at nine. In winter it must wait till afternoon.
And yet it seems a bigger place, and by tradition the temple
priests from Kedarnath winter there when the snows cover
that distant shrine.

Guptakashi has not yet been rendered ugly by the
barrack type architecture that has come up in some growing
hill towns. The old double-storeyed houses are built of
stone, with grey slate roofs. They blend well with the
hillside. Cobbled paths meander through the old bazaar.

One of these takes up to the famed Guptakashi temple,
tucked away above the old part of the town. Here, as in
Benares, Shiva is worshipped as Vishwanath, and two
underground streams representing the sacred Jumna and
Bhagirathi rivers feed the pool sacred to the god. This
temple gives the town its name—Gupta-Kashi, the 'Invisible
Benares', just as Uttarkashi on the Bhagirathi is 'Upper
Benares'.

Guptakashi and its environs has so many lingams that
the saying *Jitne kankar utne Shankar*—'as many stones,
so many Shivas'—has become a proverb to describe its
holiness.

From Guptakashi, pilgrims proceed north to Kedarnath,
and the last stage of their journey—about a day's march—
must be covered on foot or horseback. The temple of
Kedarnath, situated at a height of 11,753 ft, is encircled by
snow-capped peaks, and Atkinson has conjectured that 'the

Kedarnath Temple

symbol of the linga may have arisen from the pointed peaks around his (God Shiva's) original home'.

The temple is dedicated to Sadashiva, the subterranean form of the god, who, 'fleeing from the Pandavas took refuge here in the form of a he-buffalo and finding himself hard-pressed, dived into the ground leaving the hinder parts on the surface, which continue to be the subject of adoration.'

The other portions of the god are worshipped as follows: the arms at Tungnath, at a height of 13,000 ft; the face at Rudranath (12,000 ft); the belly at Madmaheshwar, eighteen miles north-east of Guptakashi; and the hair and head at Kalpeshwar, near Joshimath. These five sacred shrines form the Panch Kedars (five Kedars).

We leave the Mandakini to visit Tungnath on the Chandrashila range. But I will return to this river. It has captured my mind and heart.

The Magic of Tungnath

THE MOUNTAINS AND VALLEYS OF GARHWAL NEVER FAIL
to spring surprises on the traveller in search of the
picturesque. It is impossible to know every corner of the
Himalayas, which means that there are always new corners
to discover; forest or meadow, mountain stream or wayside
shrine.

The temple of Tungnath, at a little over 12,000 ft, is the
highest shrine on the inner Himalayan range. It lies just
below the Chandrashila peak. Some way off the main
pilgrim routes it is less frequented than Kedarnath or
Badrinath, although it forms a part of the Kedar temple
establishment. The priest here is a local man, a Brahmin
from the village of Maku; the other Kedar temples have
South Indian priests, a tradition begun by Sankaracharya,
the eighth century Hindu reformer and revivalist.

Tungnath's lonely eminence gives it a magic of its own. To get there (or beyond it), one passes through some of the most delightful temperate forests in the Garhwal Himalayas. Pilgrim or trekker or just plain rambler, such as myself, one comes away a better man, forest-refreshed, and more aware of what the earth was really like before mankind began to strip it bare.

Duiri Tal, a small lake, lies cradled on the hill above Ukhimath at a height of 8,000 ft. It was the favourite spot of one of Garhwal's earliest British Commissioners, J.H. Batten, whose administration continued for twenty years (1836-56). He wrote: 'The day I reached there it was snowing and young trees were laid prostrate under the weight of snow, the lake was frozen over to a depth of about two inches. There was no human habitation, and the place looked a veritable wilderness. The next morning when the sun appeared, the Chaukhamba and many other peaks extending as far as Kedarnath seemed covered with a new quilt of snow as if close at hand. The whole scene was so exquisite that one could not tire of gazing at it for hours. I think a person who has a subdued settled despair in his mind would all of a sudden feel a kind of bounding and exalting cheerfulness which will be imparted to his frame by the atmosphere of Duiri Tal.'

This feeling of uplift can be experienced almost anywhere along the Tungnath range. Duiri Tal is still some way way off the beaten track, and anyone wishing to spend the night there should carry a tent; but further along this range, the road ascends to Dugalbeta (at about 9,000 ft) where a PWD rest house, gaily painted, has come up like some exotic orchid in the midst of a lush meadow topped by excelsia pines and pencil cedars. Many an official who has stayed here has rhapsodised on the charms of Dugalbeta; and if you are unofficial (and therefore not entitled to stay in the bungalow), you can move on to Chopta, lusher still, where there is accommodation of a sort for pilgrims and other hardy souls. Two or three little tea-shops provide mattresses and quilts. The Garhwal Mandal Vikas Nigam has put up a rest house. These tourist rest houses, scattered over the length and breadth of Garhwal, are a great boon to travellers; but during the pilgrims season (May/June), they are filled to overflowing, and if you turn up unexpectedly, you might have to take your pick of tea-shop or 'dharamsala', something of a lucky dip, since they vary a good deal in comfort and cleanliness.

The trek from Chopta to Tungnath is only three and a half miles, but in that distance one ascends about 3,000 ft and the pilgrim may be forgiven for feeling that at places he is on a perpendicular path. Like a ladder to heaven, I couldn't help thinking.

In spite of its steepness, my companion, the redoubtable climber Ganesh Saili, insisted that we take a short cut. After clawing our way up tufts of alpine grass, which formed the rungs of our ladder, we were stuck and had to inch our way down again, so that the ascent of Tungnath began to resemble a game of Snakes and Ladders.

Tungnath Temple

A tiny guardian-temple dedicated to Lord Ganesh surprised on top. Nor was I really fatigued; for the cold fresher air and the verdant greenery surrounding us was like an intoxicant. Myriads of wild flowers grew on the open slopes—buttercups, anemones, wild strawberries, forget-me-nots, rock-cross, enough to rival Bhyunders' Valley of Flowers at this time of the year.

But before reaching these alpine meadows, we climb through a rhododendron forest, and here one finds at least three species of this flower: the red-flowering tree rhododendron (found throughout the Himalayas between 6,000 ft and 10,000 ft); a second variety, the Almatta, with flowers that are light red or rosy in colour; and the third, Chimul or white variety, found at heights ranging between 10,000 ft and 13,000 ft. The Chimul is a brushwood, seldom more than twelve feet high and growing slantingly due to the heavy burden of snow it has to carry for almost six months in a year.

The brushwood rhododendrons are the last trees on our ascent, for as we approach Tungnath, the treeline ends and there is nothing between the earth and the sky except grass and rock and tiny flowers. Above us, a couple of crows dive-bomb a hawk, who does his best to escape their attentions. Crows are the world's great survivors. They are capable of living at any height and in any climate; as much at home in the back streets of Delhi as on the heights of Tungnath.

Another surviver, up here at any rate, is the Pika, a sort of mouse-hare, who looks neither like a mouse nor a hare but rather like a tiny guinea-pig; small ears, no tail, grey-brown fur, and chubby feet. They emerge from their holes under the rock to forage for grasses on which to feed. Their simple diet and thick fur enable them to live in extreme cold, and they have been found at 16,000 ft, which is higher than where any mammal lives. The Garhwalis call this little creature the Runda—at any rate, that's what the temple priest called it, adding that it was not averse to entering houses and helping itself to grain and other delicacies. So perhaps there's more in it of mouse than of hare.

These little Rundas were with us all the way from Chopta to Tungnath, peering out from their rocks or scampering about on the hillside, seemingly unconcerned by our presence. At Tungnath they live beneath the temple flagstones. The priest's grandchildren were having a game discovering their burrows; the Rundas would go in at one hole and pop at another; they must have had a system of underground passages.

When we arrived, clouds had gathered over Tungnath, as they do almost every afternoon. The temple looked austere in the gathering gloom.

To some, the name 'tung' indicates 'lofty', from the position of the temple on the highest peak outside the main chain of the Himalayas; others derive it from the word 'tangna'— 'to be suspended'—in allusion to the form under which the deity is worshipped here. The form is the Swayambhu Ling; and on Shivratri or the night of Shiva, the true believer may, 'with the eye of faith', see the lingam increase in size; but 'to the evil-minded no such favour is granted'.

The temple, though not very large, is certainly impressive, mainly because of its setting and the solid slabs of grey granite from which it is built. The whole place somehow reminds me of Emily Bronte's *Wuthering Heights*—bleak, wind-swept, open to the skies. And as you look down from the temple at the little half-deserted hamlet that serves it in summer, the eye is met by grey slate roofs and piles of stones, with just a few hardy souls in residence, for the majority of pilgrims new prefer to spend the night down at Chopta.

Even the temple priest, attended by his son and grandsons, complains bitterly of cold. To spend every day barefoot on those cold flagstones must indeed be a hardship. I wince after five minutes of it, made worse by stepping into a puddle of icy water. I shall never make a good pilgrim; no reward for me in this world or the next. But the pandit's feet are literally thick-skinned, and the children seem oblivious to the cold. Still, in October they must be happy to descend to Maku, their home village on the slopes below Dugalbeta.

It begins to rain as we leave the temple. We pass herds of sheep huddled in the ruined dharamsala. The crows are still rushing about the grey weeping skies, although the hawk has very sensibly gone away. A Runda sticks his nose out from his hole, probably to take a look at the weather. There is a clap of thunder and he disappears, like the white rabbit in *Alice in Wonderland*. We are halfway down the Tungnath 'ladder' when it begins to rain quite heavily. And now we pass our first genuine pilgrims, a group of intrepid Bengalis who are heading straight into the storm. They are without umbrellas or raincoats, but they are not to be deterred.

Oaks and rhododendrons flash past as we dash down the steep, winding path. Another short cut, and rock-climber Ganesh Saili takes a tumble, but is cushioned by moss and buttercups. My wristwatch strikes a rock and the glass is shattered. No matter. Time here is of little or no significance. Away with time! Is this, I wonder, the 'bounding and exciting cheerfulness' experienced by Batten and now manifesting itself in me?

The tea-shop beckons. How would one manage in the hills without these wayside tea-shops? Miniature inns, they provide food, shelter, and even lodging to dozens at a time.

We sit on a bench between a Gujar herdsman and a pilgrim who is too feverish to make the climb to the temple. He accepts my offer of an aspirin to go with his tea. We tackle some buns—rock-hard, to match our environment— and wash the pellets down with hot sweet tea.

There is a small shrine here, too, right in front of the tea-shop. It is a slab or rock roughly shaped like a lingam, and it is daubed with vermilion and strewn with offerings of wild flowers. The mica in the rock gives it a beautiful sheen.

I suppose Hinduism comes closest to being a nature religion.

Rivers, rocks, trees, plants, animals and birds, all play their part, both in mythology and in everyday worship. This harmony is most evident in these remote places, where god and mountains co-exist. Tungnath, as yet unspoilt by a materialistic society, exerts its magic on all who come here with open mind and heart.

The Road to Badrinath

IF YOU HAVE TRAVELLED UP THE MANDAKINI VALLEY, AND then cross over into the valley of the Alaknanda, you are immediately struck by the contrast. The Mandakini is gentler, richer in vegetation, almost pastoral in places; the Alaknanda is awesome, precipitous, threatening, and seemingly inhospitable to those who must live and earn a livelihood in its confines.

Even as we left Chamoli and began the steady, winding climb to Badrinath, the nature of the terrain underwent a dramatic change. No longer did green fields slope gently down to the riverbed. Here they clung precariously to rocky slopes and ledges that grew steeper and narrower, while the river below, impatient to reach its confluence with the Bhagirathi at Deoprayag, thundered along a narrow gorge.

Badrinath is one of the four Dhams, or four most holy places in India (the other three are Rameshwaram, Dwarka and Jagannath Puri). For the pilgrim travelling to his holiest of holies, the journey is exciting, possibly even uplifting; but for those who live permanently on these crags and ridges, life is harsh, a struggle from one day to the next. No wonder so many young men from Garhwal make their way into the Army. Little grows on these rocky promontories; and what does is at the mercy of the weather. For most of the year the fields lie fallow. Rivers, unfortunately, run downhill and not uphill.

The harshness of this life, typical of much of Garhwal, was brought home to me at Pipalkoti, where we stopped for the night. Pilgrims stop here by the coachload, for the Garhwal Mandal Vikas Nigam's rest house is fairly capacious and small hotels and dharamsalas abound. Just off the busy road is a tiny hospital, and here, late in the evening, we came across a woman keeping vigil over the dead body of her husband. The body had been laid out on a bench in the courtyard. A few feet away the road was crowded with pilgrims in festival mood; no one glanced over the low wall to notice this tragic scene.

The woman came from a village near Helong. Earlier that day, finding her consumptive husband in a critical condition, she had decided to bring him to the nearest town for treatment. As he was frail and emaciated, she was able to carry him on her back for several miles until she reached the motor road. Then, at some expense, she engaged a

Badrinath Temple

passing taxi and brought him to Pipalkoti. But he was already dead when she reached the small hospital. There was no morgue; so she sat beside the body in the courtyard, waiting for dawn and the arrival of others from the village. A few men arrived next morning, and we saw them wending their way down to the cremation ground. We did not see the woman again. Her children were hungry and she had to hurry home to look after them.

Pipalkoti is hot (and pipal trees are conspicuous by their absence), but Joshimath, the winter resort of the Badrinath temple establishment, is about 6,000 ft above sea-level and has an equable climate. It is now a fairly large town, and although the surrounding hills are rather bare, it does have one great tree that has survived the ravages of time. This is an ancient mulberry, known as the Kalpa-Vriksha (Immortal Wishing Tree), beneath which the great Sankaracharya meditated a few centuries ago. It is reputedly over two thousand years old, and is certainly larger than my modest four-roomed flat in Mussoorie. Sixty pilgrims holding hands might just about encircle its trunk.

I have seen some big trees, but this is certainly the oldest and broadest of them. I am glad that Sankaracharya meditated beneath it and thus ensured its preservation. Otherwise it might well have gone the way of other great trees and forests that once flourished in this area.

A small boy reminds me that it is a Wishing Tree, so I make my wish. I wish that other trees might prosper like this

'Have you made a wish?' I ask the boy.

'I wish that you will give me one rupee,' he says.

His wish comes true with immediate effect. Mine lies in an uncertain future. But he has given me a lesson in wishing.

Joshimath has to be a fairly large place because most of Badrinath arrives here in November, when the shrine is snowbound for six months. Army and PWD structures also dot the landscape. This is no carefree hill resort, but it has all the amenities for making a short stay quite pleasant and interesting. Perched on the steep mountainside above the junction of the Alaknanda and Dhauli rivers, it is now vastly different from what it was when Frank Smythe visited it fifty years ago and described it as 'an ugly little place..... straggling unbeautifully over the hillside. Primitive little shops line the main street, which is roughly paved in places and in others has been deeply channelled by the monsoon rains. The pilgrims spend the night in single-storeyed rest houses, not unlike the hovels provided for the Kentish hop-pickers of former days, and are filthy and evil-smelling'.

Those were Joshimath's former days. It is a different place today, with small hotels, modern shops, a cinema; and its growth and comparative modernity dates from the early sixties when the old pilgrim footpath gave way to the motor road which takes the traveller all the way to Badrinath. No longer does the weary, footsore pilgrim sink gratefully down in the shade of the Kalpa-Vriksha. He alights from his bus or luxury coach and drinks a Cola or a Thums-up at one of the many small restaurants on the roadside.

Contrast this comfortable journey with the pilgrimage fifty years ago. Frank Smythe again: 'So they venture on their pilgrimage....Some borne magnificently by coolies, some toiling along in rags, some almost crawling, preyed on by disease and distorted by dreadful deformities.....Europeans who have read and travelled cannot conceive what goes on in the minds of these simple folk, many of them from the agricultural parts of India. Wonderment and fear must be the prime ingredients. So the pilgrimage becomes an adventure. Unknown dangers threaten the broad well-made path, at any moment the Gods, who hold the rocks in leash, may unloose their wrath upon the hapless passerby. To the European it is a walk to Badrinath, to the Hindu pilgrim it is far, far more.'

Above Vishnuprayag, Smythe left the Alaknanda and entered the Bhyundar valley, a botanist's paradise, which he called the Valley of Flowers. He fell in love with the lush meadows of this high valley and made it known to the world. It continues to attract the botanist and trekker. Primulas of subtle shades, wild geraniums, saxifrages clinging to the rocks, yellow and red potentillas, snow-white anemones, delphiniums, violets, wild roses, all these and many more flourish there, capturing the mind and heart of the flower-lover.

'Impossible to take a step without crushing a flower.' This may not be true any more, for many footsteps have trodden the Bhyundar in recent years. There are other areas in Garhwal where the hills are rich in flora—the Har-ki-Doon, Harsil, Tungnath, and the Khiraun valley where the Balsam grows to a height of eight feet—but the Bhyundar has both a variety and a concentration of wild flowers, especially towards the end of the monsoon. It would be no exaggeration to call it one of the most beautiful valleys in the world.

The Bhyundar is a digression for lovers of mountain scenery; but the pilgrim keeps his eyes fixed on the ultimate goal—Badrinath, where the gods dwell and where salvation is to be found.

There are still a few who do it the hard way—mostly those who have taken sanyas and renounced the world. Here is one hardy soul doing penance. He stretches himself out on the ground, draws himself up to a standing position, then flattens himself out again. In this manner he will proceed from Badrinath to Rishikesh, oblivious of the sun and rain, the dust from passing buses, the sharp gravel of the footpath.

Others are not so hardy. One saffron-robed scholar speaking fair English asks us for a lift to Badrinath, and we find a space for him. He rewards us with a long and involved commentary on the Vedas, which lasts through the remainder of the journey. His special field of study, he informs us, is the part played by Aeronautics in Vedic literature.

'And what,' I ask him, 'is the connection between the two?'

He looks at me pityingly.

'It is what I am trying to find out,' he replies.

The road drops to Pandukeshwar and rises again, and all the time I am scanning the horizon for the forests of the Badrinath region I had read about many years ago in Eraser's *Himalaya Mountains*. Walnuts growing up to 9,000 ft, deodars and Bilka up to 9,500 ft, and Amesh and Kiusu fir to a similar height—but, apart from strands of long leaved and excelsia pine, I do not see much, certainly no deodars. What has happened to them, I wonder. An endless variety of trees delighted us all the way from Dugalbeta to Mandal, a well-protected area, but here on the high ridges above the Alaknanda, little seems to grow: or, if ever anything did, it has long since been bespoiled or swept away.

Finally we reach the windswept, barren valley which harbours Badrinath—a growing township, thriving, lively, but somewhat dwarfed by the snow-capped peaks that tower above it. As at Joshimath, there is no dearth of hostelries and dharamsalas. Even so, every hotel or rest house is overcrowded. It is the height of the pilgrim season, and pilgrims, tourists and mendicants of every description throng the river-front.

Just as Kedar is the most sacred of the Shiva temples in the Himalayas, similarly Badrinath is the supreme place of worship for the Vaishnav sects.

According to legend, when Sankaracharya in his Digvijaya travels visited the Mana valley, he arrived at the Narada-Kund and found fifty different images lying in its waters. These he rescued, and when he had done so, a voice from Heaven said: These are the images for the Kaliyug, establish them here.' Sankaracharya accordingly placed them beneath a mighty tree which grew there and whose shade extended from Badrinath to Nandprayag, a distance of over eighty miles. Close to it was the hermitage of Nar-Nandprayag (or Arjuna and Krishna), and in course of time temples were built in honour of these   and   other manifestations of Vishnu. It was here that Vishnu appeared to his followers in person, as four-armed, crested and adorned with pearls and garlands. The faithful, it is said, can still see him on the peak of Nilkantha, on the great Kumbha day. It is in fact the Nilkantha peak that dominates this crater-like valley, where a few hardy thistles and nettles manage to survive. Like cacti in the desert, the pricklier forms of life seem best equipped to live in a hostile environment.

Nilkantha means blue-necked, an allusion to Lord Shiva's swallowing of a poison meant to destroy the world. The poison remained in his throat, which was rendered blue thereafter. It is a majestic and awe-inspiring peak, soaring to a height of 21,640 ft. As its summit is only five miles from Badrinath, it is justly held in reverence. From its ice-clad pinnacle, three great ridges sweep down, of which the south terminates in the Alaknanda valley.

On the evening of our arrival we could not see the peak, as it was hidden in cloud. Badrinath itself was shrouded in mist. But we made our way to the temple, a gaily decorated building, about fifty feet high, with a gilded roof. The image of Vishnu, carved in black stone, stands in the centre of the sanctum, opposite the door, in a Dhyana posture. An endless stream of people pass through the temple to pay homage and emerge the better for their proximity to the divine.

From the temple, flights of steps lead down to the rushing river and to the hot springs which emerge just above it. Another road leads through a long but tidy bazaar where pilgrims may buy mementos of their visit—from sacred amulets to pictures of the gods in vibrant technicolour. Here at last I am free to indulge my passion for cheap rings, with none to laugh at my foible. There are all kinds, from rings designed like a coiled serpent (my favourite) to twisted bands of copper and iron and others containing the pictures of gods, gurus and godmen. They do not cost more than two or three rupees each, and so I am able to fill my pockets. I never wear these rings. I simply hoard them away. My friends are convinced that in a previous existence I was a jackdaw, seizing upon and hiding away any kind of bright and shiny object!

India is a land of crowds, and it is no different at Badrinath where people throng together, all in good spirits. Hindus enjoy their religion. Whether bathing in cold streams or hot springs, or tramping from one sacred mountain shrine to another, they are united in their wish to experience something of the magic and mystique of the gods and glories of another epoch.

Even those who have renounced the world appear to be cheerful—like the young woman from Gujarat who had taken sanyas, and who met me on the steps below the temple. She gave me a dazzling smile and passed me an exercise book. She had taken a vow of silence; but being, I think, of an extrovert nature, she seemed eager to remain in close communication with the rest of humanity, and did so by means of written questions and answers. Hence the exercise book. Together we filled three pages of it before she told me that she wished to proceed on pilgrimage to Amarnath but was short of funds. With help from my generous companion, we made her a donation, and with a flashing smile of thanks she left us and was lost in the crowd.

Although at Badrinath I missed the sound of birds and the presence of trees, there were other compensations. It was good to be part of the happy throng at its colourful little temple and to see the sacred river close to its source. And early next morning I was rewarded with the loveliest experience of all.

Opening the window of my room and glancing out, I saw the rising sun touch the snow-clad summit of Nilkantha. At first the snows were pink; then they turned to orange and gold. All sleep vanished as I gazed up in wonder at that magnificent pinnacle in the sky. And had Lord Vishnu appeared just then on the summit, I would not have been in the least surprised.

Where Rivers Meet

IT IS A FUNNY THING, BUT LONG BEFORE I ARRIVE AT A PLACE I can usually tell whether I am going to like it or not. Thus, while I was still some twenty miles from the town of Pauri, I felt it was not going to be my sort of place, and sure enough, it wasn't. On the other hand, while Nandprayag was still out of sight, I knew I was going to like it. And I did.

Perhaps it's something on the wind—emanations of an atmosphere—that are carried to me well before I arrive at my destination! I can't really explain it. And no doubt it's silly to be prejudiced in advance. But it happens that way, and I mention the fact for what it's worth.

As for Nandprayag, perhaps I'd been there in some previous existence, because I felt I was nearing home as soon as we drive into this cheerful roadside hamlet, some little way above the Mandakini's confluence with the Alaknanda. A prayag is a meeting place of two rivers, and since there are many rivers in Garhwal, all linking up to join either the Ganga or the Jumna, it follows that there are numerous prayags, in themselves places of pilgrimage as well as wayside halts en route to the shrines at Kedarnath and Badrinath. Nowhere else in the Himalayas are there so many temples, sacred streams, holy places and holy men. Truly this is the kingdom of the gods—so much so that the mortal rulers of these mountain tracts have left but little mark of their own in the history of the region. Every little place is steeped in religious mythology. It was as though the Pandavas bestrode these mountains only yesterday. And perhaps they did, if we consider the premise that it isn't time passing—only you and I !

Some little way above Nandprayag's busy little bazaar is the tourist rest house, perhaps the nicest of their rest houses in this area. It has a pretty garden surrounded by fruit trees and is some distance from the general hubbub of the main road.

Above it is the old pilgrim road, on which you walked, for let us remember that just over twenty years ago, if you were a pilgrim intent on finding salvation at Badrinath or Kedarnath, you went on foot all the way from Rishikesh—and in the process covered a few hundred miles in a couple of months. They had the time, they had the faith, they had the endurance. Illness and misadventure often dogged their footsteps, but what was a little suffering if at the end of it they arrived at the very portals of Heaven! Some did not survive to make the return journey. Today's pilgrims may not be lacking in devotion, but most of them do expect to come home again.

Along the old pilgrim path are several handsome old houses set amongst mango trees and the fronds of the papaya and banana. Higher up the hill the pine forests can be seen, but down here it is almost sub-tropical. Nandprayag is about 3,000 ft above sea-level—a height at which the vegetation is usually quite lush, provided there is protection from the wind, as there is here.

In one of these double-storeyed houses lives Mr Devki Nandan Vaishnav, scholar and recluse. He welcomes me into his home and plies me with food till I am close to bursting. He has a great love for his little corner of Garhwal and proudly shows me his collection of clippings concerning Nandprayag. One of them is from a book by Sister Nivedita, the Englishwoman Margaret Noble, who embraced Hinduism. Writing in 1928, she had this to say:

> Nandprayag is a place that ought to be famous for its beauty and order. For a mile or two before reaching it we had noticed the superior character of the agriculture and even some careful gardening of fruits and vegetables. The peasantry also suddenly grew handsome, not unlike the Kashmiris. The town itself is new, rebuilt since the Gohna flood, and its temple stands far out across the fields on the shore of the Prayag. But in this short time, a wonderful energy has been at work on architectural carvings,

and the little place is full of gemlike beauties. Its temple is dedicated to Naga Takshaka. As the road crosses the river, I noticed two or three old Pathan tombs, absolutely the only trace of Mohammedanism that we had seen north of Srinagar (Garhwal).

Little has changed since Sister Nivedita's time, and there is still a small Pathan population in Nandprayag. In fact, when I called on Mr Vaishnav, he was in the act of sending out Id greetings to his Muslim friends. Some of the old graves have disappeared in the debris from new road cuttings. And as for the beautiful temple described by Sister Nivedita, I was sad to learn that it had been swept away by a mighty flood in 1970, when a cloudburst and landside at Belakuchi on the Alaknanda resulted in great destruction downstream.

Mr Vaishnav remembers the time when he walked to Pauri to join the old Messmore mission school, where so many famous sons of Garhwal received their early education. It took him four days to get there. Now it is just four hours by bus. It was only after the Chinese invasion of 1962 that there was a rush of road-building in the hill districts of northern India. Before that, everyone walked and thought nothing of it.

Sitting alone that same evening in the little garden of the rest house, I heard innumerable birds break out in song. I do not see any of them, because the trees are dark and the light is fading, but there is the rather melancholy call of the hill dove, the insistent ascending trill of the koel, and much shrieking, whistling and twittering that I am unable to assign to any particular species. Oh, that Salim Ali were here with me!

And now, once again, while I sit on the lawn surrounded by zinnias, I am assailed by that feeling of having been here before. Here, on this lush hillside, among the pomegranates and oleanders. Is it some childhood memory asserting itself? But as a child I came no further than Rishikesh. Nandprayag has some affinity with parts of the Doon valley before the Doon was submerged by a tidal wave of humanity, but in the Doon there is no great river running past your garden, and here there are two, and they are also part of this feeling of belonging. So perhaps in some previous existence, I did come this way, a pilgrim or some sort of flower person? Or perhaps I lived and belonged here, which accounts for the familiarity. Who knows? And anyway, mysteries are more interesting than certainties.

Presently the room-boy joins me for a chat on the lawn. He is in fact running the rest house in the absence of the manager. A coachload of pilgrims is due at any moment, but until they arrive the place is empty and only the birds can be heard. His name is Janakpal, and he tells me something about his village on the next mountain where a leopard has been carrying off goats and cattle. He doesn't think much of the law protecting leopards: nothing can be done about it unless the leopard becomes a man-eater!

A shower of rain descends on us, and so do the pilgrims; Janakpal leaves me to attend to his duties. But I am not left alone for long. A youngster with a cup of tea appears. He wants me to take him to Mussoorie or Delhi. He is fed up, he says, with washing dishes in Nandprayag.

'You are better off here,' I tell him sincerely. 'In Mussoorie you will have twice as many dishes to wash. In Delhi, ten times as many.'

'But there are cinemas and video there,' he says, and I am left without an argument.

The rain stops and I go for a walk. The pilgrims keep to themselves, but the locals are always ready to talk. So I am not alone for long. I remember a saying (and it may have originated in Garhwal), which goes: All men are my friends. I have only to meet them.' In the hills, where life still moves at a leisurely and civilised pace, one is constantly meeting them.

The Mussoorie cinemas having all closed, Janakpal moved to Delhi but found that ticket prices were beyond his reach.

Ganga Descends

THERE HAS ALWAYS BEEN A MILD SORT OF CONTROVERSY as to whether the true Ganga (in its upper reaches) is the Alaknanda or the Bhagirathi. Of course the two rivers meet at Deoprayag and then both are Ganga. But there are some who assert that geographically the Alaknanda is the true Ganga, while others say that tradition should be the criterion, and traditionally the Bhagirathi is the Ganga.

I put the question to my friend Dr Sudhakar Misra, from whom words of wisdom sometimes flow; and true to form, he answered: The Alaknanda is Ganga, but the Bhagirathi is Ganga-ji.'

One sees what he means. The Bhagirathi is beautiful, almost caressingly so, and people have responded to it with love and respect, ever since Lord Shiva released the waters of the goddess from his locks and she sped plainswards in the tracks of Prince Bhagirath's chariot.

The Revered Goddess

'He held the river on his head,
And kept her wandering, where,
Dense as Himalayas' woods were spread,
The tangles of his hair.'

Revered by Hindus, and loved by all, the Goddess Ganga weaves her spell over all who come to her. Moreover, she issues from the very heart of the Himalayas. Visiting Gangotri in 1820, the writer and traveller Baillie Fraser noted: 'We are now in the centre of the Himalayas, the loftiest and perhaps the most rugged range of mountains in the world.'

Perhaps it is his realisation that one is at the very centre and heart of things that gives one an almost primaeval sense of belonging to these mountains, and to this river valley in particular. For me, and for many who have been in the mountains, the Bhagirathi is the most beautiful of the four main river valleys of Garhwal. It will remain so provided we do not pollute its waters and strip it of its virgin forests.

The Bhagirathi seems to have everything—a gentle disposition, deep glens and forests, the ultravision of an open valley graced with tiers of cultivation leading up by degrees to the peaks and glaciers as its head.

From some twenty miles above Tehri, as far as Bhatwari, a distance of fifty-five miles along the valley, there are extensive forests of pine. It covers the mountains on both sides of the rivers and its affluents, filling the ravines and plateaus up to a height of about 5,000 ft. Above Bhatwari, forests of box, yew and cypress commence, and if we leave the valley and take the roads to Nachiketa Tal or Dodi Tal— little lakes at around 9,000 ft above sea-level—we pass through dense forests of oak and chestnut. From Gangnani to Gangotri, the deodar is the principal tree. The Sp. excelsia pine also extends eight miles up the valley above Gangotri, and birch is found in patches to within half a mile of the glacier.

On the right bank of the river, above Sukni, the forest is nearly pure deodar, but on the left bank, with a northern aspect, there is a mixture of silver-fir, spruce, and birch. The valley of the Jadganga is also full of deodar, and towards its head the valuable pencil cedar is found. The only other area of Garhwal where the deodar is equally extensive is the Jaunsar Bawar tract to the west.

It was the valuable timber of the deodar that attracted the adventurer Frederic 'Pahari' Wilson to the valley in the 1850s. He leased the forests from the Raja of Tehri in 1859 for a period of five years. In that short span of time he made a fortune.

The old forest rest houses at Dharasu, Bhatwari and Harsil were all built by Wilson as staging posts, for the only roads were narrow tracks linking one village to another. Wilson married a local girl, Gulabi, from the village of Mukhba, and the portraits of the Wilsons (early examples of the photographer's art) still hang in these sturdy little bungalows. At any rate, I found their pictures at Bhatwari.

Harsil is now out of bounds to civilians, and I believe part of the old house was destroyed in a fire a few years ago. This sturdy building withstood the earthquake which devastated the area in 1991.

Amongst other things, Wilson introduced the apple into this area, 'Wilson apples'—large, red and juicy—sold to travellers and pilgrims on their way to Gangotri. This fascinating man also acquired an encyclopaedic knowledge of the wildlife of the region, and his articles, which appeared in *Indian Sporting Life* in the 1860s, were later plundered by so-called wildlife writers for their own works.

Bridge-building was another of Wilson's ventures. These bridges were meant to facilitate travel to Harsil and the Shrine at Gangotri. The most famous of them was a 350 ft suspension bridge over the Jatganga at Bhaironghat, over 1200 ft above the young Bhagirathi, where it thunders through a deep defile. This rippling contraption of a bridge was at first a source of terror to travellers, and only a few ventured across it. To reassure people, Wilson would often mount his horse and gallop to and fro across the bridge. It has since collapsed, but local people will tell you that the hoofbeats of Wilson's horse can still be heard on full-moon nights. The supports of the old bridge were complete tree-trunks, and they can still be seen to one side of the new motor-bridge built by engineers of the Northern Railway.

Wilson's life is fit subject for a romance; but even if one were never written, his legend would live on, as it has done for over a hundred years. There has never been any attempt to commemorate him, but people in the valley still speak of him in awe and admiration, as though he had lived only yesterday. Some men leave a trail of legend behind them because they give their spirit to the place where they have lived, and remain forever a part of the rocks and mountain streams.

In the old days, only the staunchest of pilgrims visited the shrines at Gangotri and Jamnotri. The roads were rocky and dangerous, winding along in some places, ascending and descending the faces of deep precipices and ravines, at times leading along banks of loose earth where landslides had swept the original path away. There are still no large towns above Uttarkashi, and this absence of large centres of population may be reason why the forests are better preserved than those in the Alaknanda valley, or further downstream.

Gangotri is situated at just a little over 10,300 ft. On the right bank of the river is the Gangotri temple, a small neat building without too much ornamentation, built by Amar Singh Thapa, a Nepali General, early in the nineteenth century. It was renovated by the Maharaja of Jaipur in the 1920s. The rock on which it stands is called Bhagirath Shila and is said to be the place where Prince Bhagirath did penance in order that Ganga be brought down from her abode of eternal snow.

Here the rocks are carved and polished by ice and water, so smooth that in places they look like rolls of silk. The fast flowing waters of this mountain torrent look very

Gangotri Temple

different from the huge sluggish river that finally empties its waters into the Bay of Bengal fifteen hundred miles away.

The river emerges from beneath a great glacier, thickly studded with enormous loose rocks and earth. The glacier is about a mile in width and extends upwards for many miles. The chasm in the glacier through which the stream rushed forth into the light of day is named Gaumukh, the cow's mouth, and is held in deepest reverence by Hindus. The regions of eternal frost in the vicinity were the scene of many of their most sacred mysteries.

The Ganga enters the world no puny stream, but bursts from its icy womb a river thirty or forty yards in breadth. At Gauri Kund (below the Gangotri temple) it falls over a rock of considerable height and continues tumbling over a succession of small cascades until it enters the Bhaironghati gorge.

A night spent beside the river, within the sound of the fall, is an eerie experience. After some time it begins to sound, not like one fall but a hundred, and this sound permeates both one's dreams and waking hours. Rising early to greet the dawn proved rather pointless at Gangotri, for the surrounding peaks did not let the sun in till after 9 a.m. Everyone rushed about to keep warm, exclaiming delightedly at what they call 'gulabi thand', literally, 'rosy cold'. Guaranteed to turn the cheeks a rosy pink! A charming expression, but I prefer a rosy sunburn, and remained beneath a heavy quilt until the sun came up to throw its golden shafts across the river.

This is mid-October, and after Diwali the shrine and the small township will close for winter, the pandits retreating to the relative warmth of Mukbha. Soon snow will cover everything, and even the hardy purple-plumaged whistling thrushes, lovers of deep shade, will move further down the valley. And down below the forest-line, the Garhwali farmers go about harvesting their terraced fields which form patterns of yellow, green and gold above the deep green of the river.

Yes, the Bhagirathi is a green river. Although deep and swift, it does not lose its serenity. At no place does it look hurried or confused—unlike the turbulent Alaknanda, fretting and frothing as it goes crashing down its boulder-strewn bed. The Alaknanda gives one a feeling of being trapped, because the river itself is trapped. The Bhagirathi is free-flowing, easy. At all times and places it seems to find its true level.

Uttarkashi, though a large and growing town, is as yet uncrowded. The seediness of towns like Rishikesh and parts of Dehra Dun is not yet evident here. One can take a leisurely walk through its long (and well-supplied) bazaar, without being jostled by crowds or knocked over by three-wheelers. Here, too, the river is always with you, and you must live in harmony with its sound as it goes rushing and humming along its shingly bed.

Uttarkashi is not without its own religious and historical importance, although all traces of its ancient town of Barahat appear to have vanished. There are four important temples here, and on the occasion of Makar Sankranti, early in January, a week-long fair is held when thousands from the surrounding areas throng the roads to the town. To the beating of drums and blowing of trumpets, the gods and goddesses are brought to the fair in gaily decorated palanquins. The surrounding villages wear a deserted look that day as everyone flocks to the temples and bathing ghats and to the entertainments of the fair itself.

We have to move far downstream to reach another large centre of population, the town of Tehri, and this is a very different place from Uttarkashi. Tehri has all the characteristics of a small town in the plains—crowds, noise, traffic congestion, dust and refuse, scruffy dhabas—with this difference that here it is all ephemeral, for Tehri is destined to be submerged by the water of the Bhagirathi when the Tehri dam is finally completed.

The rulers of Garhwal were often changing their capitals, and when, after the Gurkha War (of 1811-15), the former capital of Srinagar became part of British Garhwal, Raja Sudershan Shah established his new capital at Tehri. It is said that when he reached this spot, his horse refused to go any further. This was enough for the king, it seems; or so the story goes.

Perhaps Prince Bhagirath's chariot will come to a halt here too, when the dam is built. The two hundred and forty-six metre high earthen dam, with forty-two square

Kalimath Temple

miles of reservoir capacity, will submerge the town and about thirty villages.

But as we leave the town and cross the narrow bridge over the river, a mighty blast from above sends rocks hurtling down the defile, just to remind us that work is indeed in progress.

Unlike the Raja's horse, I have no wish to be stopped in my tracks at Tehri. There are livelier places upstream. And as for Ganga herself, that deceptively gentle river, I wonder if she will take kindly to our efforts to contain her.

Great Trees of Garhwal

LIVING FOR MANY YEARS IN A COTTAGE AT 7,000 FT IN THE Garhwal Himalayas, I was fortunate to have a big window that opened out on the forest, so that the trees were almost within my reach. Had I jumped, I should have landed quite safely in the arms of an oak or chestnut.

The incline of the hill was such that my first floor window opened on what must, I suppose, have been the second floor of the tree. I never made the jump, but the big langurs—silver grey monkeys with long swishing tails—often leapt from the trees onto the corrugated tin roof and made enough noise to disturb the bats sleeping in the space between the roof and ceiling.

Standing on its own was a walnut tree, and truly this was a tree for all seasons. In winter the branches were bare; but they were smooth and straight and round like the arms of a woman in a painting by Jamini Roy. In the spring, each branch produced a hard, bright spear of new leaf. By midsummer the entire tree was in leaf; and towards the end of the monsoon, the walnuts, encased in their green jackets, had reached maturity.

Then the jackets began to split, revealing the hard brown shell of the walnuts. Inside the shell was the nut itself. Look closely at the nut and you will notice that it is shaped rather like the human brain. No wonder the ancients prescribed walnuts for headaches!

Every year the tree gave me a basket of walnuts. But last year the walnuts were disappearing one by one, and I was at a loss to know who had been taking them. Could it have been Bijju, the milkman's son? He was an inveterate tree climber. But he was usually to be found on oak trees, gathering fodder for his cows. He told me that his cows liked oak leaves but did not care for walnuts. He admitted that they had relished my dahlias, which they had eaten the previous week, but he denied having fed them walnuts.

It wasn't the woodpecker. He was out there every day, knocking furiously against the bark of the tree, trying to prise an insect out of a narrow crack. He was strictly non-vegetarian and none the worse for it.

One day I found a fat langur sitting in the walnut tree. I watched him for some time to see if he was going to help himself to the nuts, but he was only sunning himself. When he thought I wasn't looking, he came down and ate the geraniums; but he did not take any walnuts.

The walnuts had been disappearing early in the morning while I was still in bed. So one morning I surprised everyone, including myself, by getting up before sunrise. I was just in time to catch the culprit climbing out of the walnut tree.

She was an old woman, who sometimes came to cut grass on the hillside. Her face was as wrinkled as the walnuts she had been helping herself to. In spite of her age, her arms and legs were sturdy. When she saw me, she was as swift as a civet cat in getting out of the tree.

'And how many walnuts did you gather today, Grandmother?' I asked.

'Only two,' she said with a giggle, offering them to me on her open palm. I accepted one of them. Encouraged, she climbed back into the tree and helped herself to the remaining nuts. It was impossible to object. I was taken up in admiration of her agility in the tree. She must have been about sixty, and I was a mere forty-five, but I knew I would never be climbing trees again.

To the victor the spoils !

The horse chestnuts are inedible, even the monkeys throw them away in disgust. Once, on passing beneath a horse chestnut tree, a couple of chestnuts bounched off my head. Looking up, I saw that they had been dropped on me by a couple of mischievous rhesus monkeys.

The tree itself is a friendly one, especially in summer when it is full leaf. The least breath of wind makes the leaves break into conversation, and their rustle is a cheerful sound, unlike the sad notes of pine trees in the wind. The spring flowers look like candelabra, and when the blossoms fall they carpet the hillside with their pale pink petals.

We pass now to my favourite tree, the deodar. In Garhwal and Kumaon it is called Dujar or Devdar; in Jaunsar and parts of Himachal it is known as the Kelu or Kelon. It is also identified with the cedar of Lebanon (the cones are identical), although the deodar's needles are slightly longer and more bluish. Trees, like humans, change with their environment. Several persons familiar with the deodar at Indian hill-stations, when asked to point it out in London's Kew Gardens, indicated the cedar of Lebanon; and when shown a deodar, declared that they had never seen this tree in the Himalayas!

We shall stick to the name deodar, which comes from the Sanskrit *Deva-daru* (divine tree). It is a sacred tree in the Himalayas; not worshipped, not protected in the way that a peepul is in the plains, but sacred in that its timber has always been used in temples, for doors, windows, walls and even roofs. Quite frankly, I would just as soon worship the deodar as worship anything, for in its beauty and majesty it represents Nature in its most noble aspect.

No one who has lived amongst deodars would deny that it is the most godlike of Himalayan trees. It stands erect, dignified; and though in a strong wind it may hum and sigh and moan, it does not bend to the wind. The snow slips softly from its resilient branches. In the spring the new leaves are tender green, while during the monsoon the tiny young cones spread like blossoms in the dark green folds of the branches. The deodar thrives in the rain and enjoys the company of its own kind. Where one deodar grows, there will be others. Isolate a young tree and it will often pine away.

The great deodar forests are found along the upper reaches of the Bhagirathi valley and the Tons in Garhwal; and in Himachal and Kashmir, along the Chenab and the Jhelum, and also the Kishenganga; it is at its best between 7,000 and 9,000 ft. I had expected to find it on the upper reaches of Alaknanda, but could not find a single deodar along the road to Badrinath. That particular valley seems hostile to trees in general, and deodars in particular.

The average girth of the deodar is 15-20 ft, but individual trees often attain a great size. Records show that one great deodar was 250 ft high, 20 ft in girth at the base, and more than five hundred and fifty years old. The timber of these trees, which is unaffected by extremes of climate, was always highly prized for house buildings; and in the villages of Jaunsar Bawar, finely carved doors and windows are a feature of the timbered dwellings. Many of the quaint old bridges over the Jhelum in Kashmir are supported on pillars fashioned from whole deodar trees; some of these bridges are more than five hundred years old.

To return to my own trees, I went among them often, acknowledging their presence with the touch of my hand against their trunks—the walnut's smooth and polished; the pine's patterned and whorled; and oak's rough, gnarled, full of experience. The oak had been there the longest, and the wind had bent his upper branches and twisted a few, so that he looked shaggy and undistinguished. It is a good tree for the privacy of birds, its crooked branches spreading out with no particular effect; and sometimes the tree seems uninhabited until there is a whirring sound, as of a helicopter approaching, and a party of long-tailed blue magpies stream across the forest glade.

After the monsoon, when the dark red berries had ripened on the hawthorn, this pretty tree was visited by green pigeons, the kokla birds of Garhwal, who clambered upside-down among the fruit-laden twigs. And during winter, a white-capped redstart perched on the bare branches of the wild pear tree and whistled cheerfully. He had come down from higher places to winter in the garden.

The pines grow on the next hill—the chir, the Himalayan blue pine, and the long leaved pine—but there is a small blue pine a little way below the cottage, and sometimes I sit beneath it to listen to the wind playing softly in its branches.

Open the window at night and there is usually something to listen to: the mellow whistle of a pigmy owlet, or the cry of a barking deer which has scented the proximity of a panther. Sometimes, if you are lucky, you will see the moon coming up over Nag Tibba and two distant deodars in perfect silhouette.

Some sounds cannot be recognised. They are strange night sounds, the sounds of the trees themselves, stretching their limbs in the dark, shifting a little, flexing their fingers. Great trees of the mountains, they know me well. They know my face in the window; they see me watching them, watching them grow, listening to their secrets, bowing my head before their outstretched arms and seeking their benediction.

Birdsong in the Hills

BIRD-WATCHING IS MORE DIFFICULT IN THE HILLS THAN ON the plains. Many birds are difficult to spot against the dark green of the trees or the varying shades of the hillsides. Large gardens and open fields make bird-watching much easier on the plains; but up here in the mountains one has to *he* quick of eye to spot a flycatcher flitting from tree to tree, or a mottled brown treecreeper ascending the trunk of oak or spruce. But few birds remain silent, and one learns of their presence from their calls or songs. Birdsong is with you wherever you go in the hills, from the foothills to the tree line; and it is often easier to recognise a bird from its voice than from its colourful but brief appearance.

The barbet is one of those birds which are heard more than they are seen. Summer visitors to our hill-stations must have heard their monotonous, far-reaching call, *pee-oh, pee-oh,* or *un-nee-ow, un-nee-ow.* They would probably not have seen the birds, as they keep to the tops of high trees where they are not easily distinguished from the foliage. Apart from that, the sound carries for about half a mile, and as the bird has the habit of turning its head from side to side while calling, it is very difficult to know in which direction to look for it.

Barbets love listening to their own voices and often two or three birds answer each other from different trees, each trying to outdo the other in a shrill shouting match. Most birds are noisy during the mating season. Barbets are noisy all the year round!

Some people like the barbet's call and consider it both striking and pleasant. Some don't like it and simply consider it striking!

In parts of the Garhwal Himalayas, there is a legend that the bird is the reincarnation of a moneylender who died of grief at the unjust termination of a law suit. Eternally his plaint rises to heaven, *un-nee-ow, un-nee-ow!* which means, 'injustice, injustice'.

Barbets are found throughout the tropical world, but probably the finest of these birds is the great Himalayan barbet. Just over a foot in length, it has a massive yellow bill, almost as large as that of a toucan. The head and neck are a rich violet; the upper back is olive brown with pale green streaks. The wings are green, washed with blue, brown and yellow. In spite of all these brilliant colours, the barbet is not easily distinguished from its leafy surroundings. It goes for the highest treetops and seldom comes down to earth.

Barbet

Hodgson's grey-headed flycatcher-warbler is the long name that ornithologists, in their infinite wisdom, have given to a very small bird. This tiny bird is heard, if not seen, more often than any other bird throughout the Western Himalayas. It is almost impossible to visit any hill-station between Naini Tal and Dalhousie without noticing this warbler; its voice is heard in every second tree; and yet there are few who can say what it looks like.

Its song (if you can call it that) is not very musical, and Douglas Dewar in writing about it was reminded of a notice that once appeared in a third-rate music hall: The audience is respectfully requested not to throw things at the pianist. He is doing his best.

Our little warbler does his best, incessantly emitting four or five unmusical but joyful and penetrating notes.

He is much smaller than a sparrow, being only some four inches in length, of which one-third consists of tail. His lower plumage is bright yellow, his upper parts olive green; the head and neck are grey, the head being set off by cream-coloured eyebrows. He is an active little bird always on the move, and both he and his mate, and sometimes a few friends, hop about from leaf to leaf, looking for insects both large and small. And the way he puts away an inch long caterpillar would please the most accomplished spaghetti eater!

Another tiny bird more often than it is seen is the green-backed tit, a smart little bird about the size of a sparrow. It constantly utters a sharp, rather metallic but not unpleasant, call which sounds like 'kiss me, kiss me, kiss me...'

Another fine singer is the sunbird, which is found in Kumaon and Garhwal. But perhaps the finest songster is the grey-winged ouzel. Throughout the early summer he makes the wooded hillsides ring with his blackbird-like melody. The hill people call this bird the Kastura or Kasturi, a name also applied to the Himalayan whistling thrush. But the whistling thrush has a yellow bill, whereas the ouzel is red-billed and is much the sweeter singer.

Nightjars (or goatsuckers, to give them their ancient name) are birds that lie concealed during the day in shady woods, coming out at dusk on silent wings to hunt for insects. The nightjar has a huge frog-like mouth, but is best recognised by its long tail and wings and its curiously silent flight. After dusk and just before dawn, you can hear its curious call, *tonk-tonk, tonk-tonk*—a note like that produced by striking a plank with a hammer.

As we pass from the plains to the hills, the traveller is transported from one bird realm to another.

Rajpur is separated from Mussoorie by a five mile footpath, and within that brief distance we find the caw of the house crow replaced by the deeper note of the corby. Instead of the crescendo shriek of the koel, the double note of the cuckoo meets the ear. For the eternal cooing of the little brown dove, the melodious kokla green pigeon is substituted. The harsh cries of the rose-ringed parakeets give place to the softer call of the slate-headed species. The dissonant voices of the seven sisters no longer issue from

Mountain Thrush

the bushes; their place is taken by the weird but more pleasing calls of the Himalayan streaked laughing-thrushes.

When I first came to live in the hills, it was the song of the Himalayan whistling thrush that caught my attention. I did not see the bird that day. It kept to the deep shadows of the ravine below the old stone cottage.

The following day I was sitting at my window, gazing out at the new leaves on the walnut and wild pear trees. All was still, the wind was at peace with itself, the mountains brooded massively under the darkening sky. And then, emerging from the depths of that sunless chasm like a dark sweet secret, came the indescribably beautiful call of the whistling thrush.

It is a song that never fails to thrill and enchant me. The bird starts with a hesitant schoolboy whistle, as though trying out the tune; then, confident of the melody, it bursts into full song, a crescendo of sweet notes and variations that ring clearly across the hillside. Suddenly the song breaks off right in the middle of a cadenza, and I am left wondering what happened to make the bird stop so suddenly.

At first the bird was heard but never seen. Then one day I found the whistling thrush perched on the broken garden-fence. He was deep glistening purple, his shoulders flecked with white; he has sturdy black legs and a strong yellow beak. A dapper fellow who would have looked just right in a top hat! When he saw me coming down the path, he uttered a sharp *kree-ee*—unexpectedly harsh when compared to his singing—and flew off into the shadowed ravine.

As the months passed, he grew used to my presence and became less shy. Once the rain water pipes were blocked, and this resulted in an overflow of water and a small permanent puddle under the steps. This became the whistling thrush's favourite bathing place. On sultry summer afternoons, while I was taking a siesta upstairs, I would hear the bird flapping about in the rainwater pool. A little later, refreshed and sunning himself on the roof, he would treat me to a little concert—performed, I could not help feeling, especially for my benefit.

It was Govind, the milkman, who told me the legend of the whistling thrush, locally called Kastura by the hill people, but also going by the name of Krishan-patti.

According to the story, Lord Krishna fell asleep near a mountain stream and while he slept, a small boy made off with the god's famous flute. Upon waking and finding his flute gone, Krishna was so angry that he changed the culprit into a bird. But having once played on the flute, the bird had learnt bits and pieces of Krishna's wonderful music. And so he continued, in his disrespectful way, to play the music of the gods, only stopping now and then (as the whistling thrush does) when he couldn't remember the tune.

It wasn't long before my whistling thrush was joined by a female, who looked exactly like him. (I am sure there are subtle points of difference, but not to my myopic eyes!) Sometimes they gave solo performances, sometimes they sang duets; and these, no doubt, were love calls, because it wasn't long before the pair were making forays into the rocky ledges of the ravine, looking for a suitable maternity home. But a few breeding seasons were to pass before I saw any of their young.

After almost three years in the hills, I came to the conclusion that these were 'birds for all seasons'. They were liveliest in midsummer; but even in the depths of winter, with snow lying on the ground, they would suddenly start singing, as they flitted from pine to oak to naked chestnut.

As I write, there is a strong wind rushing through the trees and bustling about in the chimney, while distant thunder threatens a storm. Undismayed, the whistling thrushes are calling to each other as they roam the wind-threshed forest.

Whistling thrushes usually nest on rocky ledges near water; but my overtures of friendship may have my visitors other ideas. Recently I was away from Mussoorie for about a fortnight. When I returned, I was about to open the window when I noticed a large bundle of ferns, lichen, grass, mud and moss balanced outside on the window ledge. Peering through the glass, I was able to recognise this untidy bundle as a nest.

It meant, of course, that I couldn't open the window, as this would have resulted in the nest toppling over the edge. Fortunately the room had another window and I kept this one open to let in sunshine, fresh air, the music of birds, and, always welcome, the call of the postman! The postman's call may not be as musical as birdsong, but this writer never tires of it, for it heralds the arrival of the occasional cheque that makes it possible for him to live close to nature.

And now, this very day, three pink freckled eggs lie in the cup of moss that forms the nursery in this jumble of a nest. The parent birds, both male and female, come and go, bustling about very efficiently, fully prepared for a great day that's coming soon.

The wild cherry trees, which I grew especially for birds, attract a great many small birds, both when it is in flower and when it is in fruit.

When it is covered with pale pink blossoms, the most common visitor is a little yellow-backed sunbird, who emits a squeaky little song as he flits from branch to branch. He

Paradise Flycatcher

extracts the nectar from the blossoms with his tubular tongue, sometimes while hovering on the wing but usually while clinging to the slender twigs.

Just as some vegetarians will occasionally condescend to eat meat, the sunbird (like the barbet) will vary his diet with insects. Small spiders, caterpillars, beetles, bugs and flies (probably in most cases themselves visitors to these flowers), fall prey to these birds. I have also seen a sunbird flying up and catching insects on the wing.

The flycatchers are gorgeous birds, especially the paradise flycatcher with its long white tail and ghostlike flight; and although they are largely insectivorous, like some meat-eaters they will also take a little fruit! And so they will occasionally visit the cherry tree when its sour little cherries are ripening. While travelling over the boughs, they utter twittering notes with occasional louder calls, and now and then the male bird breaks out into a sweet little song, thus justifying the name of Shah Bulbul by which he is known in northern India.

Early Plant Collectors

THE FACT THAT THE HIMALAYAS HAD ALWAYS BEEN closed to travellers and botanists from Europe only intensified the desire to explore them. Towards the end of the eighteenth century, the barriers seemed to be giving way a little, and Thomas Bogle was able to travel, in 1774, to Lhasa through Bhutan; William Kirkpatrick, in 1793, was received at Nayakot in Nepal; and Thomas Hardwicke went in 1796 on a political mission to the ruler of Garhwal at Srinagar in the Alaknanda valley.

Thomas Hardwicke (1757-1835) was a soldier who, along with Claude Martin (who founded the Martiniere schools), collected plants around Lucknow and Kanpur in early days. Hardwicke was chiefly a zoologist but was also an active botanist. He was the first European to collect in the north-western Himalaya. This he did on his mission to

Garhwal—a journey which he described in *Asiatic Researches* (1799).

The plains depended so much on rivers from the hills for irrigating crops that there was a need for exploring the sources of the Ganga and the Jumna. Arrangements were made to send surveyors into the mountains of Garhwal, and a permit was obtained from the Gurkhas who had recently over-run that part of the Himalayas. The expedition was led by William Spencer Webb, an officer of Engineers and a surveyor of the first rank. He had two companions—the Anglo-Indian soldier Hyder Jung Hearsey and Felix Vincent Raper. They reached Jumnotri, where the sources of the Jumna spring; and they fixed the position of Gangotri where the Ganga has its source; but they were hurried out of the mountains by the Gurkhas.

This expedition did not have any important botanical results, but it showed William Moorcroft (1765-1825), the Bengal Government's veterinary officer, what might be done. Without permission, and with the adventurous Hearsey as a companion, he passed beyond the sources of the Ganga, over the Niti Pass and right to the sources of the Sutlej in the Manasoravar Lakes. They brought back a bundle of dried plants, which was sent to London; these were the first plants obtained from far back in the mountains. Soon afterwards, the British found themselves at war with the Gurkhas, and when peace came again (1816), the Gurkhas had withdrawn their claim to Kumaon and Garhwal.

This was the prelude to much plant-collecting. Robert Blinkworth and Bharat Singh collected in Nepal and the north-west Himalaya; and in 1818, the first seed of *Rhododendron arboreum* was sent to Britain. Blinkworth spent most of his life in the Himalayas.

Residents were placed where trade-routes emerged from the north-west Himalayas—one at Dehra Dun, another at Nahan and a third at Sabathu. The station of Dehra Dun gave birth to the more elevated station of Mussoorie, and the station of Sabathu to the station of Simla, a little higher. In 1827, the Governor-General, Lord Amherst, set the seal of approval on Simla by deciding to spend the hot weather there, and in due course it became the summer capital of British India.

In 1820, Lord Hastings visited Saharanpur. There he had been shown an old but neglected garden, once the garden of Zabita Khan, son of the more famous Najib-ud-Daula. Hastings restored it, and it soon became an important centre for promoting the knowledge of the flora of the hills. Early surveyors also used Saharanpur as a base. It was then a very small place which Jacquemont, writing in 1830, called 'truly a pleasant place... one of the pleasantest English stations in India'. He would not recognise this teeming city today, were his spirit to come this way again.

William Spencer Webb (1784-1865) and the three brothers—Alexander Gerard (1792-1839), James Gilbert Gerard (1794-1828) and Parick Gerard (1795-1835)—

did much arduous travelling in remote places and collected plants along the watershed of the Sutlej. Their names are commemorated in the coniferous trees, *Abies webbiana* and *Pinus gerardiana*

In France, the leader of scientific thought was the renowned Baron Cuvier, and he was not satisfied with the efforts made by his countrymen to get scientific information from India. He persuaded Victor Jacquemont (1801-32), a young man of 'wonderful vitality and attractiveness', to undertake a prolonged period of travelling.

Jacquemont arrived in Calcutta in May 1829, and was given every facility for study at the Calcutta Botanical Garden (then in the charge of Sir Charles Metcalfe), a garden that he called a 'magnificent establishment'. The letters that he wrote home *(Letters from India,* translated into English in 1935), and the diary printed by the Government of France in 1841, give a delightful picture of Calcutta life. When the monsoon rains were over, Jacquemont proceeded up-country to Saharanpur where he was made welcome by John Forbes Royle, the specialist in medicinal plants, who was now in charge of the Botanical Garden.

Jacquemont spent the summer in the mountains. He went through Dehra Dun and Mussoorie to the sources of the Jumna and the Tons; then to Simla; then to Spiti, and back to Delhi. This was his first season of continuous collecting.

Among the French officers employed by Ranjit Singh, the Sikh ruler of the Punjab, was General Allard. It was through his influence that Jacquemont obtained permission to enter Kashmir, being the first botanist to do so. He spent the summer of 1831 in the valley or in the hills that surround it, and at the end of the summer, made his way back to Delhi with a great collection. But his health had not been able to stand up to the rigours of the journey, and he died at Bombay in December, only thirty-one years old. His collection of plants was forwarded to Paris.

Not all these early plant-collectors were botanists. But the spirit of enquiry was common to all of them. They were seekers of knowledge. And there were many like Jacquemont, who were prepared to risk their health and even their lives in the pursuit of knowledge.

White Clouds, Green Mountains

TOWARDS THE END OF SEPTEMBER, THOSE FEW MONSOON clouds that still linger over the Himalayas are no longer burdened with rain and are able to assume unusual shapes and patterns, chasing each other across the sky and disappearing in spectacular sunset formations.

I have always found this to be the best time of the year in the hills. The sun-drenched hillsides are still an emerald green; the air is crisp, but winter's bite is still a month or two away; and for those who still like to take to the open road on foot, there are springs, streams and waterfalls tumbling over rocks that remain dry for most of the year. The lizard that basked on a sun-baked slab of granite last May is missing, but in his place the spotted forktail trips daintily among the boulders in a stream; and the strident sound of the cicadas is gradually replaced by the gentler trilling of the crickets and grasshoppers.

Cicadas, as you probably know, make their music with their legs, which are moved like the bows of violins against their bodies. It's rather like an orchestra tuning up but never quite getting on with the overture or symphony. Aunt Ruby, who is a little deaf, can nevertheless hear the cicadas when they are at their loudest. She lives not far from a large boarding-school, and one day when I remarked that I could hear the school choir or choral group singing, she nodded and remarked: 'Yes, dear. They do it with their legs, don't they?'

Come to think of it, that school choir does sound a bit squeaky.

Now, more than at any other time of the year, the wildflowers come into their own.

The hillside is covered with a sward of flowers and ferns. Sprays of wild ginger, tangles of clematis, flat clusters of yarrow and lady's mantle. The datura grows everywhere with its graceful white balls and prickly fruits. And the wild woodbine provides the stems from which the village boys make their flutes.

Aroids are plentiful and attract attention by their resemblance to snakes with protruding tongues—hence the popular name, cobra lily. This serpent's tongue is a perfect landing-stage for flies etc., who, crawling over the male flowers in their eager search for the liquor that lies at the base of the spike (a liquor that is most appealing to their depraved appetites), succeed in fertilising the female flowers as they proceed. We see that it is not only humans who become addicted to alcohol. Bears have been known to get drunk on the juice of rhododendron flowers, while bumble bees can be out-and-out dipsomaniacs.

One of the more spectacular cobra lilies, which rejoices in the name *Sauromotum Guttatum* — ask your nearest botanist what that means!—bears a solitary leaf and purple spathe. When the seeds form, it withdraws the spike underground; and when the rains are over and the soil is not too damp, it sends it up again covered with scarlet berries. In the opinion of the hill folk, the appearance of the red spike is more to be relied on as a forecast of the end of the monsoon than any meteorological expertise. Up here on the ranges that fall between the Jumna and the Bhagirathi (known as the Rawain), we can be perfectly sure of fine weather a fortnight after the fiery spike appears.

But it is the commelina, more than any other Himalayan flower, that takes my breath away. The secret is in its colour—a pure pristine blue that seems to reflect the deepest blue of the sky. Towards the end of the rains it appears as if from nowhere, graces the hillside for the space of about two weeks, and disappears again until the following monsoon.

When I see the first commelina, I stand dumb before it and the world stands still while I worship. So absorbed do I become in its delicate beauty that I begin to doubt the reality of everything else in the world.

But only for a moment. The blare of a truck's horn reminds me that I am still lingering on the main road leading out of the hill-station. A cloud of dust and blasts of diesel fumes are further indications that reality takes many different forms, assailing all my senses at once! Even my commelina seems to shrink from the onslaught. But as it is still there, I take heart and leave the highway for a lesser road.

Soon I have left the clutter of the town behind. What did Aunt Ruby say the other day? 'Stand still for five minutes, and they will build a hotel on top of you.'

Wasn't it Lot's wife who was turned into a pillar of salt when she looked back at the doomed city that had been her home? I have an uneasy feeling that I will be turned into a pillar of cement if I look back, so I plod on along the road to Devsari, a kindly village in the valley. It will be some time before 'developers' and big money boys get here, for no one will go to live where there is no driveway!

A tea-shop beckons. How would one manage in the hills without these wayside tea-shops? Miniature inns, they provide food, shelter, and even lodging to dozens at a time.

I tackle some buns that have a pre-Independence look about them. They are rock-hard, to match the environment, but I manage to swallow some of the jagged pieces with the hot sweet tea, which is good.

The Dehra I Know

FORMALLY, IT'S KNOWN AS DEHRA DUN, BUT IN THE 1940s and '50s, when we were young, everyone called it Dehra.

That's where I spent much of my childhood, boyhood, and early manhood, and it was the Dehra I wrote about in many of my books and stories.

It was very different from the Dehra Dun of today— much smaller, much greener, considerably less crowded; sleepier too, and somewhat laid-back, easy-going; fond of gossip, but tolerant of human foibles. A place of bicycles and pony-drawn tongas. Only a few cars; no three-wheelers. And you could walk almost anywhere, at any time of the year, night or day.

The Dehra I knew really fell into three periods. The Dehra of my childhood, staying in my grandmother's house on the Old Survey Road (not much left of that bungalow now). The Dehra of my schooldays, when I would come home for the holidays to stay with my. mother and stepfather—a different house on almost every visit, right up until the time I left for England. And then the Dehra of my return to India, when I lived on my own in a small flat above Astley Hall and wrote many of my best stories.

While I was in England, I wrote my first novel *The Room on the Roof,* which was ail about the Dehra I had left and the people and young friends I had known and loved. It was a little immature, but it came straight from the heart— the heart and mind of a seventeen-year-old—and if it's still fresh today, fifty years after its first publication, it's probably because it was so spontaneous and unsophisticated.

Back in Dehra, I wrote a sequel of sorts, *Vagrants in the Valley.* It wasn't as good, probably because I had exhausted my adolescence as a subject for fiction; but it did capture aspects of life in Dehra and the Doon valley in the early fifties.

I had returned to India and Dehra when I was twenty-one, and set up my writing shop, so to speak, in that flat above Bibiji's provision store.

Bibiji was my stepfather's first wife. He and my mother had moved to Delhi, leaving Bibiji with the provision store. I got on very well with her and helped her with her accounts, and she gave me the use of her rooms above the shop. I think it's only in India that you could find such a situation— a young offspring of the Raj, somewhat at odds with his mother and Indian stepfather, choosing to live with the latter's abandoned first wife!

Bibiji made excellent parathas, shalgam (turnip) pickle, and kanji, a spicy carrot juice. And so, romantic though I may have been, I was far from being the young poet starving in a garret, nor was Bibiji to be pitied. She was Dehra's first woman shopkeeper, and she managed very well.

Bibiji was of course much older than me; heavily built, strong. She could toss sacks of flour about the shop. Her son, rather mischievous, kept out of her reach; a cuff about the ears would send him sprawling. She suffered from a hernia, and was immensely grateful to me for bringing her a hernia-belt from England; it provided her with considerable relief.

Early morning she would march off to the mandi to get her provisions (rice, atta, pulses, etc.) wholesale, and occasionally I would accompany her. In this way I learnt the names of different pulses and lentils—moong, urad, malka, arhar, masoor, channa, lobia, rajma, etc. But I've never been tempted to write a cook book or run a ration-shop of my own.

I was quite happy cooking up stories, most of them written after dark by the light of a kerosene lantern. Bibiji hadn't been able to pay the flat's accumulated electricity bills, and as a result the connection had been cut. But this did not bother me. I was quite content to live by candlelight or lamplight. It lent a romantic glow to my writing life.

And a lot of romance went into those early stories. There was the girl on the train in 'The Eyes Are Not Here', and the girl selling baskets on the platform at Deoli, and Aunt Maram's amours behind the Dilaram Bazaar, and romantic episodes in places as unlikely as Shamli and Bijnor (Pipalnagar). However, as my intention is to give the reader a picture of Dehra as I knew it, the stories in this collection are all set in Dehra Dun and its immediate environs. I was writing for anyone who would read me. It was only much later that I began writing for children.

Some favourite places for my fictional milieu were the parade-ground or maidaan, the Paltan Bazaar and its offshoots, the lichee gardens of Dalanwala, the tea-gardens, the quiet upper reaches of the Rajpur Road (non-transformed into shopping malls), the sal forests near Rajpur, the approach to Dehra by road or rail, and of course the railway station which is much the same as it used to be.

When I was a boy, many of the bungalows (such as the one built by my grandfather) had fairly large grounds or compounds—flower gardens in front, orchards at the back. Apart from lichees, the common fruit trees were papaya, guava, mango, lemon, and the pomalo, a sort of grapefruit. Most of those large compounds have now been converted into housing-estates. Dehra's population has gone from fifty thousand in 1950 to over seven lakhs at present. Not much room left for fruit trees!

Some of the stories, such as 'A Handful of Nuts' and 'Living Without Money', were written long after I'd left Dehra, but I think the atmosphere of the place comes through quite strongly in them. When a writer looks back at a particular place or period in his life, he tries to capture the essence of the place and the experience.

During the two years I freelanced from Bibiji's flat (1956-58), I produced over thirty short stories, a couple of novellas, and numerous articles of an ephemeral nature. I managed to sell some of the stories to the BBC's Home service programme—*The Thief, Night Train at Devli, The Woman on Platform 8, The Kitimaber*—others to the *Elizabethan, Illustrated Weekly of India, Sunday Statesman* (over the years, a few have been lost.) In India, Rs 50 was the most you got for a short story or article, but you could live quite comfortably on three or four hundred rupees a month—provided your mode of transport was limited to the bicycle. Only successful businessmen and doctors owned cars.

My stepfather was an exception. He was an unsuccessful businessman who used a different car every month. That was because, before leaving Dehra, he ran a motor workshop, and if a car was left with him for repairs or overhauling ('oiling and greasing' he called it) he would use it for a month or two on the pretext of trying it out, before returning it to its owner. This he would do only when the owner's patience had reached its limit; sometimes the car had to be taken away by force. Occasionally my stepfather would relent and return the car of his own accord—along with a bill for having looked after it for so long!

His talents went unappreciated in Dehra. When he moved to Delhi he became a successful salesperson.

Some of the characters in my Dehra stories were fictional, some were based on real people; Granny was real, of course. And so were the boys in The Room' and 'Vagrants'. But did Rusty really make love to Meena Kapoor? It's a question I have often been asked and must leave unanswered. It might have happened. And then again, it might not. I prefer to leave it as a sweet mystery that will never be solved.

One thing is certain. Dehra played an integral part in my development as a writer. More than Shimla, where I did my schooling. More than London, where I lived for nearly four years. More than Delhi, where I spent a number of years. As much as Mussoorie, where I have passed half my life. It must have been the ambience of the place, something about it, that suited my temperament.

But it's a different place now, and no longer do I feel like 'singin' in the rain' as I walk down the Rajpur Road. I am in danger of being knocked down by a speeding vehicle if I try out my old song-and-dance routine. So I keep well to the side of the pavement and look out for known landmarks—an old peepal tree, a familiar corner, a surviving bungalow, a bookshop, the sabzi-mandi, a bit of wasteland where once we played cricket.

There was a wild flower, a weed, that grew all over Dehra and still does. We called it Blue Mint. It grows in ditches, in neglected gardens, anywhere there's a bit of open land. It's there nearly all the year round. I've always associated it with Dehra. The burgeoning human population has been unable to suppress it. This is one plant that will never go extinct. It refuses to go away. I have known it since I was a boy, and as long as it's there I shall know that a part of me still lives in Dehra.

Made in the USA
Middletown, DE
02 December 2020

25969145R00078